Sleepless in
San Francisco

Sleepless in San Francisco

A Ravenous Romance™ Panamour™ Original Publication

Ryan Field

A Ravenous Romance™ Panamour™ Original Publication
www.ravenousromance.com

Sleepless in San Francisco
Copyright © 2009 by Ryan Field

Ravenous Romance™
100 Cummings Center
Suite 123A
Beverly, MA 01915

ISBN-13: 978-1-60777-844-8

This book is a work of fiction, and any resemblance to persons living or dead is purely coincidental.

Chapter One

Ed said his final goodbye on a Sunday morning in early September, one of those crisp, late summer days without a cloud in the sky. Ed and his son, Noah, had driven out to East Hampton to visit the grave of Ed's deceased partner, Jake. He had been gone for more than a year, but it didn't feel that long.

Ed stood next to Noah in front of a dark gray headstone that had a hot air balloon carved in the center, his hands clasped together and his eyebrows furrowed. Young Noah kept looking up at him with wide eyes and pinched lips. Noah's head tilted all the way back, because he was only half Ed's size. But they both had the same ash blond hair, the same slightly bowed legs, and the same strong chin.

A familiar blowing sound was approaching above their heads. There was no other sound like it. It whished and echoed and rushed. It was loud enough to make them both look up at the sky at the same time, and yet they didn't see anything at first. Noah shielded his eyes from the bright Long Island sunshine with his hand and looked to the left. Ed put his hands in his pockets and looked to the right.

A moment later, the noise grew louder. And Noah pointed to

the sky and said, "Look, Dad. They're passing right over us."

When Ed looked up and saw that a cluster of hot air balloons was crossing over the cemetery, he smiled for the first time that day. There were too many to count: hundreds. They dotted the blue sky with the colors of the rainbow, some had stripes and some were solid. From a distance, they reminded him of upside down toy spin tops suspended above tiny, dark specks. He placed his hand on Noah's shoulder and said, "I'll be damned." Then he ran his fingers through his hair and shook his head back and forth.

Noah leaned into his father's side and smiled. "Do you think it's a sign, Dad?" he asked. "Maybe Dad's trying to tell us something." He'd always called Jake "Dad," too. Noah's mother lived in France, and Jake had been the only other parent he'd known.

"I don't know, buddy," Ed said, "But if I were the kind of guy who believed in signs and things of that nature, this would be a good example of one." His deceased partner had loved hot air balloons. He was always bugging Ed to go for a ride in one, but Ed had a fear of heights. So Jake had gone on balloon rides with friends instead. And he'd collected small models of them for years. And now his collection was packed in boxes that were sitting in a storage unit up in the Bronx.

They stood there watching the balloons pass until the last one was completely out of sight, and then Ed took a deep breath and said, "I guess we'd better get moving, buddy. We have a plane to catch this afternoon."

They were leaving New York for good. He'd closed his veterinary practice in the Village and he'd sold the townhouse in Turtle Bay. Their house in East Hampton had been rented for a year. Without Jake around, nothing was the same anymore. And they didn't have any extended family. So he'd decided to move to San Francisco—as far away as possible—to make a fresh start.

Noah stared down at the granite headstone and frowned. He reached forward and placed his right palm on the top and held it there for a moment, then turned to his father and said, "I'll wait for you at the car, Dad."

"I'll be right there, buddy," Ed said. Evidently, ten-year-old Noah was smart enough to know he wanted to be alone for a few minutes.

When Noah was gone, he reached into his pocket and pulled out a small rock. He wasn't Jewish, but a Jewish friend of his had once told him to always leave a rock on top of a headstone when you visit a grave because it was a sign that someone had been there. And Ed knew he wouldn't be back for a long time. So he placed the rock on the headstone and said, "Take care, Jake. Thanks for the balloons this morning. I wish I'd been able to go up with you just once."

3

As he turned to leave, his eyes filled with tears. But when he looked across the lawn and saw Noah leaning against the car watching him, he tightened his lips and squared his shoulders. He had to be strong. The past year had been hard on his son. Jake had died suddenly in an automobile accident, and they were both still in shock. So he shoved his hands into his pockets, loped back to the car, and sighed.

His life felt so disorganized. It wasn't even his car. He'd borrowed it that morning from his best friend because his Range Rover had already been shipped.

A few hours later, they were back in Turtle Bay to do a final walk-through of the townhouse. Tucker, Noah's black lab, was there to greet them at the door. When his nails clicked on the wooden floors, the sound echoed through the empty rooms. Their lives had already been shipped out to the West Coast. The only things left were a stack of brown leather suitcases in the living room and a chipped soup bowl filled with water in the kitchen for Tucker.

A woman's voice called down from the second floor. "Are you guys back?"

"We're here," Ed shouted. His best friend, Lisa, was upstairs. She'd been there all morning supervising a cleaning service so Ed and Noah could drive out to East Hampton. Without her, he wasn't sure if he would have been able to survive the last year.

She came rushing down the steps, a short, thin woman with long blond hair and bright blue eyes. She wore tight jeans, a black leather Donna Karan jacket, and black high heels. When she reached the bottom step, she kissed Ed on the cheek and grabbed Noah's hand. "Can I take him out to lunch?" she asked. "It's the last time I'm going to see him for a while, and I want him all to myself."

Noah looked up and smiled. "Can we take Tucker, too?" He'd already attached a leash to the dog's collar, and Tucker was wagging his tail.

"Sure, kid," Lisa said, brushing the top of his head with her fingertips. "We can go to that little place on the avenue with the red and white umbrellas and sit outside."

"Hold on," Ed said, "I don't know if there's time. Maybe we should just wait until the cleaning guy leaves and have something at the airport." He knew they had to arrive extra early to get Tucker into his crate and safely boarded.

"But it's his last chance to have lunch here in New York, the only *real* city in the world," Lisa said.

Noah gave him a pathetic look and said, "Please."

Ed smiled. Lisa knew the move to San Francisco was the best thing for them both, but that didn't mean she was happy about it. She really did believe New York was the only *real* city in the world. "Just get back here in an hour," he said. "The plane leaves in three hours, and you're the one driving us to the airport."

Chapter Two

Jonathan Haynes never had a problem finding a boyfriend. His hair was dark brown and straight, he got up at five each morning to work out at the gym, and people often told him he reminded them of a younger Keanu Reeves. He'd always dated one man after the other without giving it a second thought, and would have continued that way if he hadn't met Mike Sanders on the beach in Provincetown the previous summer. Mike was the serious type, a handsome, refined man in his mid-thirties who was ready to settle down in a monogamous relationship. And he wanted to do this with Jonathan.

It wasn't that Jonathan wasn't ready; he just wasn't sure he wanted to settle down with Mike.

He was always honest with Mike, too. He'd never officially committed to anything but dating. But Mike was one of those guys who called all the time and devoured his entire life. He took over his Facebook page and poked him; he Tweeted him on the hour. He also owned an established public relations firm. So he had the money to buy him expensive gifts and to take him out to fantastic restaurants all over New York. But there were two inherent problems at the root of their relationship that kept Jonathan up late at night staring at the ceiling.

One problem was that Mike tended to be slightly effeminate sometimes. He wasn't a flaming queen, and his wrists weren't limp. But every now and then he did this weird, almost-curtsy thing when he met someone new. And sometimes he spoke with a lisp. This wasn't a character judgment on Jonathan's part. Some of his best friends were extremely feminine. It's just that when it came to dating, he preferred men who didn't extend their pinky fingers and didn't shave their legs every day.

The other problem with Mike was in the bedroom. They never actually slept together because Mike preferred to sleep alone. And if the sex between them had made Jonathan's mouth water like the filet mignon at Le Cirque did, Jonathan imagined that he could have fallen in love with him. Mike was tall and lean, his hair was thick and blond, and he had a massive penis. But they were both bottoms. And when Jonathan quietly pointed this problem out to him (he knew who he was) one night after dinner in late October, Mike clenched his fists and swore up and down that he was versatile in bed, and that he could indeed be an excellent top guy. Then he dropped his pants, yanked out his big penis, and told Jonathan to get undressed and bend over.

Jonathan smiled and did what he was told with a huge smile. He tore off his clothes, got down on the floor on all fours, and spread his legs as wide as they would go. He was smaller than Mike, and his body was lean and wiry. He knew how to spread his legs and arch his back in an exaggerated way that most men couldn't. When Mike grabbed his hips and pulled him back, he closed his eyes and prepared for the mount. And when Mike covered his penis with a lubricated condom and pressed the tip to his opening, he took a deep breath and sighed. It had been a while, and there were few things in life Jonathan loved more than this.

But the moment Mike entered his body, his lips turned down and he stopped arching his back. Mike didn't grab his hips and squeeze hard like some guys; he touched them lightly with the tips of his delicate fingers instead. It was just like all the other times they'd tried to do this. So while Mike tried to buck his pelvis, Jonathan opened his eyes and looked at the clock on the nightstand to see how long it would take. The time before this it had only lasted five minutes.

This was bad. Mike bucked his hips without a set rhythm; he pushed in and out with awkward jerks and painful thrusts. His penis didn't slide in and out with ease. It invaded Jonathan's body with sharp pokes and misplaced moves. And the harder he tried, the worse it became.

Three minutes later, they both climaxed and Mike pulled out. Then he smiled and said, "See? I can be a top when I have to be."

9

Jonathan raised his eyebrows and forced a smile. "Ah well, I see that," he said. But the words *when I have to be* repeated in his head for a long time.

Then late one Friday night in early October, Jonathan stumbled across an e-mail that raised his eyebrows. The subject line of the e-mail read, "Sleepless in San Francisco." Jonathan worked in television as the host of a show on a do-it-yourself home improvement channel. His show was called *Dream Away*. The premise was that people planning to do extensive home renovations sent e-mails to the producers for a chance to have their home makeover televised. The show followed each step of the project from the initial demolition to the final result. *Dream Away* was now in its fifth season, and still the number-one show on the network. Jonathan's producer usually scanned the e-mails, then forwarded the most interesting ones to him for his opinion. He thought he'd read everything, until he read this one.

Dear Dream Away,

Me and my Dad just moved to San Francisco and my Dad's changing the whole house. We used to live in New York in a really nice place, but we moved away because my other Dad died in a car accident last year. We had a lot of friends there, but we don't know anybody here. My Dad thought he'd be able to sleep better in another city. But that didn't happen. So my Dad bought this big old house without seeing it first and we moved here. This place is falling apart. The other day my dog Tucker jumped off my bed and the light on the ceiling in the room under us crashed to the floor. The bathroom floor has a hole so big you can see all the way down to the kitchen. The whole place is falling down around us. But my Dad says by the time he's done with this place, he's going to make it the best house in San Francisco.

I'm a big fan of your TV show and I wanted to let you know about what my Dad is doing in case you're interested in putting us on your show. I think my Dad would sleep better if the house wasn't so bad. I know it won't bring back my other Dad who died, but it might help. I know me and Tucker would sure sleep better if that hole wasn't in the bathroom floor. And my Dad might start to feel better again.

Sincerely,

Noah Richardson

Jonathan read the e-mail two more times, then called his producer at home and told him he wanted to fly out to San Francisco to meet with the father of the kid who had written the letter. And he wanted to do this immediately. The show was set to begin production for a new season soon, and they still hadn't found an interest-

11

ing home renovation to document. They'd received thousands of e-mails, and had narrowed the prospects down to two possibilities. One was a young family in Portland, Oregon, renovating a 1960s split level, and another was a retired couple in New England renovating a barn. But as far as Jonathan was concerned, both were as interesting as a glass of prune juice. One of the reasons his show had become number one was that the people on *Dream Away* were always just as interesting as the actual home renovations. According to his most recent contract, Jonathan had the final say as to who they would be.

When the producer pointed out to him that he didn't have an actual address in San Francisco, Jonathan waved his hand and assured him he'd get one. Then he hung up and replied to Noah's e-mail, asking for his contact information so he could speak directly with his father.

But Noah didn't reply. And Jonathan couldn't sleep that night. The thought of doing a show in San Francisco with a widowed gay father who had a young son made his heart beat so fast he could hardly close his eyes. It was relevant; it was warm; it was perfect for his viewers.

So the next morning he booked a flight, packed a bag, and took a taxi to the airport. He didn't even know where he was going until he finally landed in San Francisco and checked his BlackBerry.

He'd just sat down in a rental car when he noticed an e-mail with a subject line that read, "Sleepless in San Francisco." It was short; just an address and no telephone number.

Jonathan quickly sent a reply and asked for a phone number so he could call Noah's father. He checked out the address on his iPhone, then sat in the rental car eating chocolate for almost a half hour, waiting. But Noah never replied. So Jonathan started the engine and put the car in gear. He took a deep breath and sighed, then headed to an address located in the Forest Hill section of San Francisco.

By the time he arrived at Ed's and Noah's house, it was after seven o'clock on Saturday evening. When he clicked off the engine and opened the car door, he straightened his shoulders and walked up a long spiral path that had been laid with red pavers. He stared up at the house and smiled all the way to the door. It looked to be one of those huge, old Mission-style places built in the 1920s, with an arched portico, clay roof tiles, and beige stucco. But the shrubbery was so overgrown he couldn't see the front windows, and the lawn hadn't been mowed in weeks. He looked back and forth, up and down, and lowered his eyebrows. It was perfect for the show.

And best of all, there was a cracked sign over the front door that read, *Mi Casa de Mis Sueños*. Half of the "s" in *Casai* was missing, and the *Mis* was hanging lopsided. Jonathan's eyes opened wide and he smiled. Then he reached for a tarnished door knocker in the shape of a long, thin greyhound and tapped it three times. He spoke a little Spanish, and he knew the sign over the door translated in English to *My Dream House*.

A second later, the front door opened and a humongous black lab lunged at him. He jumped up, placed his huge paws on Jonathan's shoulders, and licked his face. A man in his middle thirties opened the door wider and looked him up and down. Then he grabbed the dog by the collar and said, "Tucker, get inside now."

The dog jumped down, lowered his head, and clomped back into the house without hesitating. Jonathan wiped dog saliva from the side of his face and said, "He sure is friendly." He loved all animals, especially dogs.

The guy frowned and said, "A little *too* friendly." He was wearing long, baggy camouflage shorts, flip flops, and a loose V-neck undershirt. His sandy blond hair was cut short and looked as if it hadn't been combed all day. It also looked as if he hadn't shaved in two or three days. But it suited him well. He didn't look unkempt, just comfortable and casual. At the end of a long, dark center hall, a little boy with wide eyes watched the man's back.

Jonathan smiled and extended his right hand. "I'm Jonathan Haynes," he said, "I'm the host of the television show *Dream Away* and I'm here about an e-mail your son sent my TV show regarding your impending home makeover. I'd like to discuss the possibility of filming the entire renovation with you for the show."

But the guy didn't reach out to shake his hand. He ran his palm through his messy hair instead and said, "I assure you I have no idea what you're talking about, buddy."

Jonathan looked past him and asked the little boy, "Are you Noah Richardson? The one who wrote the e-mail titled, 'Sleepless in San Francisco'?" Then he looked at the father and said, "I've been going back and forth with your son with e-mails about your home renovation."

The guy put his hands on his hips and looked back at his son. He lowered his voice and said, "Noah, what's this all about? Have you been e-mailing this guy?"

Noah stared for a moment, then sank into his shoulders. He slipped to the right of the doorway and disappeared with a very guilty expression on his face. The dog groaned a couple of times and followed him.

Jonathan smiled. He knew he'd have to work hard to explain all this. He was glad he'd worn his tightest jeans that day, the ones that hugged his ass and accentuated the natural arch at the small of his back. So he purposely dropped his briefcase. When he turned to pick it up again, he knew the guy was watching him. He bent down slowly and spread his legs wide. And when he rose again and turned to face him, he lowered his head and raised his large brown eyes. "I came all the way from New York just to talk to you," he said. "Won't you *please* just give me a minute of your time?" He wasn't above begging; he wanted this house on the show.

The guy took a deep breath and frowned. "You can come in for a minute," he said, "but I can tell you that I'm not interested in having my home, my life, or anything filmed on television." Then he stepped to the right and said, "I'm Dr. Ed Richardson. I'm a veterinarian."

When Jonathan stepped into the hallway and said, "It's nice to meet you, Dr. Richardson," a large white SUV pulled into the driveway and honked the horn. Noah came rushing through the hallway, carrying a backpack, and screamed, "See you tomorrow, Dad." Then he raced past them both and crossed to the SUV before Ed could grab him.

Ed waved at the man driving the SUV and shouted to Noah, "Thank you very much, Noah. We'll talk about this tomorrow." But Noah didn't hear him. He'd already jumped into the back seat and slammed the door. Ed ran his fingers through his hair again and said, "He's spending the night with a friend from school. Let's go into the living room. But I don't want to waste your time. My son shouldn't have sent you those e-mails without asking me first."

When they were in the living room, Tucker jumped up on the

sofa and rested his head on Jonathan's lap. Jonathan noticed a walnut baby grand piano in a far corner of the large room. It looked expensive. The furniture looked expensive, too, but the wallpaper was faded and torn, the floors were stained and scratched, and the only window treatments were flimsy brown shades with frayed edges. Ed sat on a white wing chair beside a walk-in fireplace made out of limestone with hand-carved swirling grapevines. Ed scolded the dog for being on the sofa, but Jonathan ran his palm down Tucker's head and said he didn't mind at all. Then he opened his briefcase and showed Ed the e-mail Noah had sent. He explained why he was there and that he wanted to begin production quickly. He also told Ed that he was so excited about filming his project that he'd actually flown out himself to see it, which was something he never did.

Ed tried to be serious, but he couldn't help laughing at Noah's e-mail. "I'm going to have a serious talk with him about this," he said. "But the kid did write a damn good letter."

"He seems like a really cool kid," Jonathan said. And he wasn't just saying it. They both seemed like decent guys.

Ed shook his head and laughed again.

Jonathan noticed his legs were slightly tanned. He should have been staring at the cracked wall over the fireplace or the scrappy floors that needed refinishing, but he couldn't take his eyes off Ed's sexy, hairy legs. They were knobby and rugged and slightly bowed. He had the urge to go down on the floor and rub his face against them. He clenched his fists and tried hard to focus on business. He was usually in control, but there was something about Ed that caused a lump in his throat and made his legs weak. His stomach had never jumped and turned so much in his life.

Ed seemed just as distracted. When he spoke to Jonathan, he stared between his eyes and his lips and didn't seem to know he was doing this. He wasn't mad anymore, but he kept repeating that his son had made a huge mistake and that he wasn't interested in having his house on the *Dream Away* television show. But his voice wasn't as firm as it should have been, and there were long, awkward pauses in the conversation that Jonathan hadn't expected.

When a police car passed the house with its siren blaring, Tucker jumped off Jonathan's lap. His briefcase flew through the air and the contents landed all over the floor near Ed. He went down on his knees to retrieve the mess, and Ed reached down to help him. Ed's legs were spread wide. There were papers next his left foot; the BlackBerry was next to his right foot. And four packages of condoms had landed on the chair, right between Ed's legs. They both reached for the papers at the same time, ignoring the condoms. Jonathan accidentally grabbed Ed's hand. Ed stopped moving. His hands were large and his fingers were thick. Jonathan squeezed harder and he didn't pull away. Ed clutched the arm of the chair with his other hand and looked him in the eye. "Tucker has a problem. He freaks out when he hears sirens. He'd chase them down the street if he wasn't in the house."

"Ah well, Dr. Richardson," Jonathan said. He wouldn't let go of his hand.

"C-call me E-ed," he stammered.

And while Tucker continued to bark and howl at the front window, Jonathan's head went down between Ed's legs and he pressed his lips to his crotch. He opened his mouth and gently bit the soft, cushiony bulge protruding through the fabric. When he closed his eyes and inhaled, Ed's camouflage shorts smelled fresh and clean. He looked up at Ed's face for a moment to see his reaction. His head was back, his eyes were closed, and his mouth was open. So he pulled down Ed's zipper and reached inside his shorts.

When he pulled his penis through the opening of his boxer shorts, Ed spread his legs wider and sat all the way back in the wing chair. His penis went from a semi-erection to a full erection in seconds. Jonathan held it in his palm and wrapped his lips around the head for a minute, then placed both his hands on Ed's thighs and swallowed the entire thing. It was about seven inches in length, but it was thicker than most. Jonathan had to open his mouth extra wide to take it all to the back of his throat. And when he pressed his tongue against the bottom of the shaft and began to suck, his mouth was so filled with flesh his cheeks barely indented at all.

But Ed's unusual girth didn't stop him from bobbing his head up and down as fast as he could. He was forced to take short breaths through his nose; his face felt hot and flushed. His hands went up under the camouflage shorts and he squeezed Ed's hairy thigh muscles hard. This was the first time in his life he'd ever felt such wild, irrepressible rush of energy with another man.

Ed must have been feeling the same way, because he grabbed the sides of Jonathan's head and lifted his face. He stared at him for a second, then stood up from the chair. When he pulled Jonathan up, he wrapped his arms around his body, and kissed him on the mouth. His chest heaved; his thick tongue filled his mouth. Jonathan rested his palms on Ed's shoulders and leaned back in his arms. Ed stopped kissing and bit his chin, then he went lower and started sucking his neck. Jonathan's head went back and his mouth fell open. Ed's heavy beard sent shocks of pleasure from his toes to his eyelids. He applied so much pressure to Jonathan's neck, there were suction noises coming from the sides of his mouth.

Jonathan finally reached down and wrapped his hand around Ed's erection, then he took a deep breath and whispered, "Don't stop."

After that, everything happened fast. Ed took complete control. He reached down to the chair for one of the lubricated condoms that had fallen out of Jonathan's briefcase and lowered him to Persian carpet on the living room floor. Then he pulled Jonathan's pants down to his ankles and rolled him over so he was face down. He pulled the cushion from the white chair and shoved it under Jonathan's stomach to lift his pelvis. It only took seconds for him to remove the condom and cover his penis. He didn't bother to remove his camouflage shorts or his V-neck undershirt; he didn't even take off his flip-flops.

When he climbed onto Jonathan's back and pressed the tip of his erection to his hole, Jonathan arched his back, stretched his left arm forward, and grabbed his own erection with his right hand. There was a brief moment of initial pain; he grabbed a handful of fringe on the carpet with his other hand and bit his bottom lip. But then Ed's penis slipped all the way into his body without a single hesitation or a moment of awkward discomfort. There was a second of pain, but it didn't last long.

Ed didn't take his time. He bucked his hips so fast, Jonathan's head wrenched up and down. But surprisingly, Ed's rhythm remained steady and even, and each time he went deep he took a deep breath and grunted. His penis stroked Jonathan's insides with such rapid sensations Jonathan began to edge before he even realized it was happening.

A few minutes later, they both climaxed at the same time: Jonathan came on the carpet and Ed filled the condom. Jonathan closed his eyes and his body went limp, then Ed rested all his weight on his back and sighed.

Chapter Three

When Jonathan finally opened his eyes again, Tucker was staring at him from the center hall. His large paws were crossed and his head tilted sideways. Jonathan winked at him, because he couldn't move. He was still pinned to the floor. Ed's wide penis was still deep in his body and his rough beard was resting on his shoulder. Tucker yawned and Jonathan closed his eyes and smiled. This was the first time in his life anyone had ever thrown him down on the floor and ravished his body.

And it was still too soon to wonder about whether or not he'd just made a colossal mistake.

Then Ed pulled out and said, "I'll be right back." He just climbed off his back and ambled out of the living room with the flip-flops clapping against the bottoms of his feet. His dick was still hanging from his pants and the condom was attached to it. He left Jonathan lying there face down with his pants around his ankles and his shirt above his waist.

By the time he returned, Jonathan had pulled up his pants, placed the cushion back on the chair and retrieved the contents of his briefcase. He was sitting on the edge of the sofa, petting Tucker's neck. He noticed Ed was carrying a roll of paper towels and a bottle of spray cleaner. His dick was back in his shorts and his zipper was up. Jonathan stared at the carpet and said, "I'm sorry I made a mess."

Ed bent over to wipe the carpet and said, "I'm sorry I lost control like that. It's not like me. You're a perfect stranger. I should know better."

"Ah well," Jonathan said. "I was a little out of control, too. Besides, we won't be perfect strangers for long if you agree to sign the contracts and do the show." He was still smiling, and he was still experiencing post-orgasmic sensations between his legs. He'd always been like that after good sex. He knew he'd feel Ed's penis in his body for the next few days.

Ed stood up and placed the towels and cleaner on the coffee table. He looked at Jonathan's neck and shook his head. "I'm sorry about the mark I left."

After the way he'd sucked his neck, Jonathan also suspected there would be a large bruise under his earlobe. But he didn't mind. He smiled and said, "I'm okay." Then he pulled the contracts out of his briefcase and said, "Now, about the show. I think this house would be perfect." He thought about waiting to mention the show again, but then decided to take an aggressive approach. He knew he it was a huge chance, but he never expected Ed to turn on him with such venom.

Ed frowned. Then he ran his fingers through his hair and said, "If you think that what just happened here between us is going to change my mind, you're sadly mistaken. This was nothing more than a quick release. I'm not interested. The last thing I need in my life is to be on a television show."

Jonathan's eyes grew wide and he clenched his fists. It sounded as if Ed was suggesting that he'd seduced him so he'd agree to do the show. "Hold on one minute, buddy," he said. "What just happened here between us has nothing to do with you being on the show. Trust me, I don't have to seduce men to get them on my show. They usually have to seduce me. Besides, *you're* the one who ripped off *my* pants, covered your hungry dick with a rubber, and fucked *my* brains out."

"Well, baby, I didn't force *you* to suck my hungry dick. And *you* certainly didn't put up much of a fight while I was fucking your brains out with that hungry dick." His voice dropped with a dark, sardonic pitch. His words were intended to hurt.

Jonathan stepped back and lowered his eyes to his shoes. Ed was mocking him, and it felt like there was a huge pit in his stomach. "That was mean," he said. "And if your intention was to hurt my feelings and degrade me, congratulations, Dr. Richardson, you've succeeded." His voice was soft and he wouldn't look at Ed's face. "You know damn well I didn't plan to seduce you on purpose. I never mix work with pleasure." Then he grabbed the contracts and shoved them into his briefcase. He just wanted to get out of there as fast as he could and never see Ed Richardson's face again.

Ed smacked his forehead with the heel of his right hand. "Hold on, Jonathan," he shouted. "I didn't mean that. I'm sorry. I'm an asshole sometimes. I know you didn't seduce me on purpose so I'd sign the contracts. I don't know why I said that." Then he sat down on the wing chair, rested his elbows on his knees, and held his head in his hands.

Jonathan took a deep breath and stopped moving. When he saw the serious expression on Ed's face, the pit in his stomach disappeared and something tugged at his heart. He knew Ed wasn't a mean man. He was a man trying to heal, but not sure how to go about doing it. So Jonathan stood there with his lips pressed together, holding the briefcase. "Look," he finally said, "I'll admit I'm dying to get this house on the show and my reasons are a little selfish. It's perfect. But now that I've met you and Noah, I also think doing the show would be the best thing for you both."

Ed sat back, folded his hands on his lap, and smiled. He tilted his head sideways and asked, "And how would doing the show be the best thing for us? I don't even know what's best for us. I moved all the way out here, and nothing's changed. I sold a wonderful home in Turtle Bay, rented out my summer house, closed my office, and left my best friend in New York."

Jonathan shrugged his shoulders and spread his arms wide. He wanted to hug him, but knew it wouldn't have been appropriate. "It would help you move on," Jonathan said. "You've obviously been through a rough time, which is understandable. But you're stuck. Noah's very worried about you. He says you hardly ever sleep. And now that I've met you both, even though I am total a stranger, I'm starting to worry about Noah. Kids are supposed to have fun, not spend their childhoods worrying about whether or not their parents sleep at night. The e-mail from Noah was a silent cry for help if I've ever seen one."

Tucker barked a few times and rubbed his head against Jonathan's leg. But he was staring at Ed.

Ed looked at him, rubbed his jaw, and said, "Sounds like Tucker agrees with you."

"I think it would be good for Noah," Jonathan said. He meant it, too. He also thought it would be the best thing for Ed, but he didn't want to say it out loud and get him mad again. Evidently, Ed was a man with a stubborn streak.

"Maybe you're right," Ed said, rubbing his jaw. "But if I do agree to do the show, I think it's important that we keep our relationship on a platonic level. I don't want any complications in my

27

life. You're a great-looking guy and all, and what happened here a few minutes ago was outrageous, but the romance part of my life is over for good."

Jonathan laughed. "I couldn't agree more," he said, "because that's the last thing I need in my life." He thought about Mike and shook his head. He was already involved in one dysfunctional relationship; he didn't need to take on Ed Richardson's baggage, too. "As far as I'm concerned, what happened between us tonight was a one-time thing, and it won't ever happen again."

He'd meant it, too. But after Ed reluctantly signed the contracts and agreed to do the show, Jonathan went back to the hotel and couldn't stop thinking about what had happened between them. Ed was right about the sex: it *had* been outrageous. But when he'd left Ed's house, Ed only shook his hand instead of kissing him goodbye.

He figured time and distance would help him forget. So Jonathan returned to New York the next day and told his producer on Monday morning that Ed had signed the contracts and that they would begin production in the Forest Hill section of San Francisco at the end of the month. The producer patted his back and took him to an expensive restaurant for lunch. He said he thought this season would be the best one they've ever done.

But Jonathan couldn't stop thinking about Ed's sexy legs

and his thick penis, no matter how hard he tried. Ed wasn't male model material, but there was something very sexy about the sum of all his parts. His mouth was a little too wide, his ears stuck out slightly, and his blond eyebrows were too thin. But he had a sexy, baseball-jock appeal that Jonathan couldn't erase from his mind. He was the kind of guy who would look just as good in black tie as he would in an old sweatshirt.

For the first time, Jonathan looked forward to Mike's predictable patterns and his conservative ways. It gave him a warm, comfortable feeling to know his safety cushion, Mike, would always be there.

Then Mike surprised him later that same week and said he'd be working out of his London office for at least six months—or maybe longer. He wasn't sure yet. Mike couldn't stop smiling when he talked about going to London. He wanted Jonathan to go with him, too. He'd taken him to a special, quiet restaurant. He held his hand, and asked him to quit his job and follow him to Europe. Then he pulled a Movado watch from his pocket and placed it on Jonathan's wrist. He promised that Jonathan would never have to worry about money again and that he'd take care of him for the rest of his life. He even said he wanted to buy a place in the Hamptons and settle down.

Jonathan held his sweet, squishy hand and thanked him, but

he told him he loved his job and he didn't want to quit for anyone or anything. He'd worked hard to make his show number one on the network. It wasn't his dream job, but it was a stepping stone toward something better. So they went back to Mike's place, had the usual sex, and promised to talk on the phone once a week while Mike was gone. And before Mike left for London, Jonathan made it perfectly clear that while he was gone, they were both free to date other people. He even offered to return the watch, but Mike insisted he keep it.

After Mike left, the month passed quickly. Jonathan owned a small studio apartment in Chelsea and he was based in New York, but he'd always wanted to buy something bigger that he could decorate with a sophisticated, shabby-chic style. A real home, with quiet crystal chandeliers, white French country chairs, and large antique armoires. But now that he could well afford a much larger place, it didn't make sense to move because he was on the road all the time. The show before Ed's he'd traveled to Vermont to film on location. And before that, he'd gone to Carmel-by-the-Sea, California, to shoot. In the past five years, he'd only spent a few months out of each year in his apartment.

This was fine with him. His place only had a full-sized brown leather bed, two French gilded end tables, and a large flat-screen television. The few pieces he owned were tasteful and expensive, but most of the time he couldn't wait to get out of his apartment and hit the road.

So it was a nice diversion when an old college friend of his called and invited him out to East Hampton the weekend before he was to leave for San Francisco. His name was Joel and he worked in the financial district. He'd rented the house for a year on a whim, because he had the money to do it. They'd both been journalism majors in college even though neither one of them had ended up working as journalists.

But more than that, Joel and Jonathan had been lovers off and on during college. They'd started out as roommates in their freshman year, then began to experiment one night. Neither one could ever remember who initiated it. Joel loved to receive good blow jobs, and Jonathan loved giving them. But their relationship never went beyond being best friends, because Joel had always considered himself straight. And he'd been married and divorced twice by the time he'd reached his mid-twenties to prove it.

When Jonathan pulled up to Joel's house in a rented car on Friday evening, he looked up the front walk and smiled. *This* was his dream house. And he'd been working on enough dream homes for other people to know what he preferred. This house had a classic, turn-of-the-century East Hampton design with gray shingles and arched gables. But the trim wasn't bright white like all the other homes that surrounded it. The trim on this house was a shade of pale blue-green that reminded him of ocean water. If he'd been designing a place of his own in East Hampton, this is exactly the color he would have painted the trim. When he crossed to the front door, he reached out and touched the pale blue-green porch railing. He ran his fingers up and down the smooth surface lightly and he smiled again.

When Joel invited him inside, the first thing Jonathan said was, "Great house. I love the color of the trim."

Joel hugged him and said, "Yeah, it's nice. I saw an extra paint can in the garage. It's called Waterbury Green. I think the owner decided to compete with Martha Stewart's house up the road, but wanted to do something really different."

"I like it better than Martha's," Jonathan said. He'd seen her house during the day and this Waterbury Green color was more subtle.

Joel led him to a glass-enclosed conservatory at the back end of the house. There were four other guys sitting around a large round table playing poker. Joel said they were buddies of his from work. They were all between the ages of twenty-five and thirty-five and they were all wearing wedding bands. The ashtrays on the table were filled with cigarette butts and a battered plastic trash can next to the table was filled with empty beer cans and folded pizza boxes. When Joel introduced Jonathan, they all howled with deep, drunken voices and asked him to join them at the table.

Jonathan loved playing cards, and poker was his favorite game. He didn't smoke and he wasn't in love with the taste of beer, but he knew how to hold his own with a deck of cards. So he wound up playing with them until three o'clock in the morning. He even won fifty dollars.

Of course he'd been expecting a long weekend alone with his good friend at a quiet time of the year in the Hamptons, where he could sit and watch the ocean and breathe in the salt air. He had been hoping he could wake up late on Saturday morning, drive into town, and stroll through the village shops on Main Street. He'd planned to jog down to the Maidstone Club and back, then drive over to Sag Harbor and take Joel out for a late lunch. But with all those other guys there for the weekend, he wasn't sure what to expect now.

Jonathan finally said goodnight and stood up from the poker table. It was well past three in the morning. But when he asked Joel where he'd be sleeping that night, one of the drunken guys reached back, grabbed his ass, and said, "My bed's free, baby." Jonathan didn't remember his name.

The guy on his other side said, "My bed's free, too," Then he put his arm around Jonathan's waist and pulled him into his lap.

Jonathan's legs went up and he had to hold his shoulders for support. He was a big, stocky guy with large biceps and a thick neck. The guy's eyes were glazed and red; his breath smelled like stale beer and tobacco. And when Jonathan tried to stand up, the guy put his hands around his waist and pinned him there. The guy laughed and said, "Why don't you get up on the table and do a little dance for us? Joel told us all about your hidden talents."

Jonathan lowered his eyebrows and gave Joel a look. Then he put his arms around the guy's shoulders, rubbed the back of his wide neck with his fingertips, and whispered, "I'll be right back, big guy. I just want to talk to Joel out in the hallway for a minute."

When they were out in the front hall, Jonathan asked, "What's going on? Who *are* these guys?"

Joel leaned into him and pushed his back to the wall. He stretched out his arms, braced his palms against the wall, and kissed him on the mouth. Jonathan's lips parted and he pressed his tongue against Joel's. He tasted familiar and smelled like spicy aftershave. His body was strong and warm. Then Joel pulled his head back and whispered, "Why don't you take off all your clothes now and go back there and surprise the guys? I told them how smooth your body is and how you give great head, and they're all so drunk and horny now they don't care about anything but getting off. They just want to get off."

"Huh?"

"You know," he said, "the same way you used to surprise me when we were in college. Do you remember that one night when me and a couple of my football buddies were studying and smoking joints, and you came out of the shower and started getting dressed in front of us? I told the guys about what you did that night. They're curious and they want you to do it again tonight."

Jonathan sighed and rolled his eyes. He'd never forget some of the things he'd done in college, especially not that night. He'd known Joel and his three buddies were stoned, and he'd seduced them all on purpose. He'd wound up on Joel's bed face down with his legs spread wide, and they'd all wound up taking turns on him. There were black and blue bruises on the backs of his legs for almost a week.

Jonathan didn't have any regrets about anything he'd done back then. But that had been college, and things were different now. So he gently kissed Joel on the cheek and said, "You know I haven't done anything like that in ages. I think I'm going back to the city now."

Joel slipped his hand down the back of his pants and grabbed his ass. He said, "I know you better than anyone else. I know you want to do this. I know how much you like dick. I'll bet it's been a long time since you've had an opportunity like this. Just put your hand between my legs. I'm as hard as a rock, and it's all because of you."

Jonathan couldn't resist his last sentence. He spread his legs wider and arched his back so Joel could play with his ass. Joel knew far too well how to make his knees weak; he had always been able to seduce him with a unique brand of dirty talk most men couldn't master.

Part of him did want to do this. The thought of taking on all those guys at once made his pulse race and brought him back to the carefree, irresponsible days of college. The fact that Joel would be there to take care of him made him feel safe. It wouldn't have been difficult for him to strip naked, tiptoe back into the conservatory, lie down on the big, round card table and take them all on at the same time.

But another part of him pulled back. So he slipped out from under Joel's arms and headed to the front door. Then he picked up his overnight bag and said, "I'm not in college anymore, Joel. I'll give you a call when I get back from San Francisco."

Joel shook his head and smiled. "Are you mad at me?"

Jonathan smiled. "Of course not. I love you. You're just a big jerk sometimes who needs to grow up."

Joel adjusted his crotch and crossed to the front door. Then he hugged him hard and said, "Drive safe, man. You know I love you, too."

He nodded. "I know that."

On the way home, Jonathan couldn't help feeling sorry for the poor bastard who had rented his house in East Hampton to Joel. He wouldn't have done that.

Chapter Four

In order to make things easier for Noah and Tucker, Ed rented a small guest house in Golden Gate Heights near Grand View Park. Lisa agreed to come out and live there while the house was under construction and the film crew was shooting. She was a marketing director for a large clothing company. When she wasn't traveling to sales meetings, she worked from home.

But it hadn't been easy explaining this to Noah, who couldn't talk about anything but the TV show and Jonathan Haynes. He'd been marking off the days on the calendar in the kitchen ever since Ed had agreed to do the show. They had the same conversation at dinner every night. "Why can't I stay here?" Noah would ask.

"Because you have school and you have to study."

"But I can study here."

"There will be too many disruptions, the whole place will be a mess, and there won't be a kitchen for a long time."

"Where will you be staying?"

"Most of the time I'll be here."

"Here?" said Noah.

"I'm doing some of the work myself to save money and speed things up."

"Jake left us millions of dollars and you don't have to save money."

"I know that, but I want to do something with my hands for a change."

This would cause Noah to frown and purposely drop a morsel of food on the floor for Tucker, and Ed would pretend he didn't see this and focus on his own plate.

In the past, Ed's deceased partner, Jake, would have moved into the guest house with Noah and Tucker and he would have turned it into a mysterious adventure. Jake had been the lighter, more nurturing of the two. He would have packed his expensive luggage, put on his darkest sunglasses, and said, "We'll move very slowly to the car, buddy, so the paparazzi won't see us." Noah's eyes would grow wide and alert, and then he'd put on his dark glasses and prepare for the dangerous journey. But now all Noah had was Ed, and all Ed could manage was a pretend smile and a sincere concern for his education. He often wondered if Noah would have been better off if he'd been the one killed in the accident instead of Jake.

On the Sunday evening before the construction began, Ed loaded Noah's bags into his Range Rover, put Tucker's dog food and bowls into a brown bag, and drove out to the airport to pick up Lisa. Then he rented her a car and they drove back to the guest house in tandem. Both Noah and Tucker rode with Lisa, because

Noah was afraid she might get lost in a new city—he was very protective when it came to Lisa. They ordered Chinese takeout because they didn't want to leave Tucker all alone in a new place the first night. And when it was time for Ed to leave, Noah lowered his eyes to his shoes and turned in the other direction. Evidently, he was still upset about not being able to stay at the house with Ed.

"I'll pick you up from school tomorrow," Ed said, touching his shoulder. "And we'll have dinner together. Okay?"

But Noah wouldn't look up. He shrugged his shoulders and folded his arms across his chest.

Lisa gave Ed a look, then smiled and put her arm around Noah's shoulder. "This is all going to go by so fast," she said, "you won't even remember how upset you are right now. And to make it a little better, you can stay up extra late tonight and we can watch TV until you fall asleep on the sofa."

"Can we watch the reruns of *Dream Away* with Jonathan Haynes?" he asked.

She smiled. "We can watch whatever you want. I'm really looking forward to this. I've been missing you since you left New York." She gave him a slight push forward and said, "C'mon, give your Dad a hug and say goodnight."

Noah stepped forward and put his arms around Ed's waist. He was still frowning, and his voice was soft, but he hugged him tight and said, "Love you, Dad."

Ed swallowed and gave Lisa look. Then he bent down and hugged him as hard as he could. "I love you, too, son."

"Just one thing, Dad," he said.

"What's that?"

"Can Lisa pick me up from school tomorrow instead of you, and take me to the house so I can see Jonathan Haynes again?"

"I'll tell you what," he said. "I'll pick you up myself so Lisa can work, and then I'll take you back to the house and you can meet the entire film crew. How's that?"

He hugged Ed harder, then smiled and said, "Sounds good."

Ed drove back to the house, hunched over the steering wheel, biting the inside of his mouth. But when he pulled into the driveway, he noticed someone crossing down the front walk. He stopped in the middle of the driveway and a man stopped walking. When he clicked off the engine and got out of the car, he saw Jonathan Haynes standing on his sidewalk. He was wearing beige jeans, a white shirt, and a charcoal sport jacket. His dark brown, almost black hair was shorter now, and he looked thinner. Before he even realized it was happening, Jonathan was crossing toward him with a huge smile on his face and his right arm extended to shake his hand. "I didn't expect to see you until tomorrow," Ed said.

Jonathan smiled. "I just wanted to stop by and see if you're all set to go tomorrow morning. Part of my job is to make sure the film crew is always in the background and you're never bothered by any of it." Then he reached out to shake his hand.

His palm was so soft and gentle, Ed felt a chill on the back of his neck. "My contractor will be here at eight, and we start demolition in the kitchen," he said. "Everything seems ready to go. And don't worry. I'm actually excited about this now."

Jonathan let go of his hand and said, "I really want this to go smoothly for you. I don't want you to have any stress because of the show. I know firsthand, after doing so many of these home renovations with other people, how stressful the construction can be sometimes."

Ed smiled again and invited him inside for coffee. They hadn't spoken since the day Ed had signed the contracts a month earlier. At first, Jonathan seemed reluctant, as if he were imposing on a school night. But when Ed told him Noah and Tucker would be living in a rented guest house with Lisa during the project, his shoulders relaxed and he agreed to go inside. They went back to the kitchen, where Ed made two fast cups of coffee in an expensive coffee maker he'd just ordered on the Internet. Jonathan sat on one side of the center island, and Ed sat on the other. They laughed about the old-fashioned 1970s wallpaper that would soon be gone. Ed said he couldn't wait to see them haul out the olive green kitchen appliances.

Jonathan leaned forward and laughed, then took a sip of coffee and said, "There's one thing I'm really curious about."

"What's that?"

"In Noah's letter he mentioned something about a hole in the bathroom," he said, "Is there really a hole?"

Ed stood from his stool and put down the coffee mug. He was wearing a black T-shirt, baggy jeans, and white running shoes. His head jerked to the back staircase and he said, "Follow me."

He jogged up the stairs and Jonathan followed him to the second floor. Then they went down a long hallway to the last door on the right. Ed led him into the master bedroom and turned left. When he reached another door, he pulled a set of keys from his pocket and unlocked a dead bolt. Then he pushed the door open, extended his right arm, and said, "See for yourself."

When Jonathan stepped into the master bathroom and looked down at the floor, his eyebrows went up and he put his hand over his mouth. "This is unbelievable," he said. He was staring down at a huge, gaping hole in the center of the bathroom floor.

Ed stood behind him and looked over his shoulder. He didn't want to get too close to the hole. Heights made his balls tighten and his stomach curl. "There was a small fire here a few years back. The former owner was an older woman. She forgot she'd left a candle burning. It was lucky she smelled smoke and called 9-1-1 when she did. They were able to contain the fire to this room and the room below it, which is the library. And there wasn't any structural damage to the house."

"Very lucky," Jonathan said, still shaking his head.

"This room is off limits," Ed said. He didn't mention his fear of heights. "I know Noah made it sound as if we actually use this bathroom, but I keep it locked at all times and use the bathroom down the hall."

Jonathan smiled. "I'm glad to hear that. I couldn't stop thinking about this hole."

Then Ed leaned forward slightly and took a deep breath. The only hole Ed had been thinking about for a month was between Jonathan's legs. It had been soft and warm and tight. His neck smelled so fresh and clean. And his aftershave reminded him of cinnamon and cloves. He looked so damn good in that black sport jacket and those beige jeans. It would have been such a shame to rip them off his back, throw him down on the floor, and spread his soft legs as wide as they would go. Ed clenched his fists and took a step back. This was wrong. Jonathan was a decent guy, and Ed had a filthy mind. Besides, he'd been the one who'd said their relationship could never be anything more than platonic.

Jonathan laughed. "This is a first for me," he said. "I've been doing this show for a long time, and I don't think I've ever seen a hole like this in anyone's bathroom."

There was a moment of silence, then Ed unclenched his right fist and rested it on Jonathan's ass. He squeezed a few times and said, "And I've never seen a hole like this between anyone's legs."

Jonathan's body tightened, as if he were terrified to move. He let Ed play with his ass for a minute, then said, "I thought we weren't going to do this again, Ed." But he didn't pull away. If anything, Ed thought he'd arched his back.

Ed stepped closer and wrapped his other arm around his waist. "I thought so, too. But you look so damn good."

Jonathan swallowed hard and said, "So do you. You smell like you've been working out. I like that."

"I should probably stop before this gets out of hand," Ed said. His middle finger was now pressing into the seam of his pants and probing the center of his ass.

"Really?"

"Do you want me to stop?"

"God, no," said Jonathan. It came out like both a sigh and a huge pressure release at the same time. He turned fast and put his arms around his shoulders. "I haven't been able to think about any-thing but you since I left here a month ago."

Ed wrapped his arms around his body and kissed him on the

mouth. When he found his soft, warm tongue, he lifted him off the floor and walked him back to the bed. The sheets were still rumpled and the pillows indented. Jake had always been the one who'd made their bed; Ed wasn't even sure how to do it. The only time it was made now was when the cleaning people came in twice a week. But when he lowered Jonathan onto the mattress and pulled off his shoes and socks, he didn't apologize—and Jonathan didn't seem to mind.

Jonathan's eyes were glazed. He pushed Ed back with his bare foot and started to remove his clothes. He literally yanked them off and tossed them into a pile at the foot of the bed. When he was naked, he opened Ed's pants, pulled down his zipper, and let them drop to his knees. Ed's penis stuck out from his pale blue boxer shorts. Jonathan grabbed it and pulled him forward. When his erection was in front of Jonathan's lips, he opened his mouth and sucked it to the back of his throat.

They moved fast, just like the last time. It was as if they'd both been deprived of food and this was their first meal in a month. Chests heaved, hearts pounded, and the sound of deep breaths rushed through the room. Jonathan gobbled and sucked him so hard, Ed saw that the side of his face had turned red and a small vein on his forehead popped out. He sucked this way until Ed was close to climax. Then Ed yanked him by the back of the head with one hand and pushed him to the middle of the bed with the other. He was so pliable and easy to maneuver; Ed could take complete control and do anything he wanted to him.

So Ed kicked off his sneakers and his jeans. He didn't care about his shirt or his socks. He opened a drawer in the nightstand and pulled out a lubricated condom. Then he climbed on top of him and kissed him on the mouth. Jonathan held his biceps, lifted his legs high, and spread them apart while they kissed. "Give it to me, Ed," he said.

A second later, Ed was inside his body, bucking his hips. He'd just shoved it in with one rough thrust, while Jonathan had shivered and moaned. He loomed over him with his palms pressed to the mattress beside Jonathan's soft shoulders, as if he were doing push-ups. Jonathan's legs were bent at the knees and spread as wide as they would go. His toes curled, his eyes rolled, and his head bounced up and down. He pressed his left hand on Ed's chest and grabbed his penis with his right. He started to jerk, while Ed continued to hammer, and moaned, "I'm so close, Ed. I don't know if I can hold back."

"Me too," Ed said. "I don't think I can hold back either."

They came at the same time. Ed grunted and Jonathan moaned, "Ah, ah, ah…" Then Ed lowered his body and rested on top of him. He cradled him in his arms and kissed him so hard their teeth clicked together.

Jonathan wrapped his legs around Ed's waist and crossed his feet at his ankles. "That was even better than the last time," he said.

He felt so good in his arms, he didn't want to let go. "It's like we have no control," Ed said. "We don't even have foreplay. We just go at it like a couple of perverted animals."

Jonathan ran his fingers across the back of Ed's neck and laughed. "Maybe we are just a couple of sex-starved perverts."

Ed thought for a moment. He had a point. Maybe this was all just pent-up lust because he hadn't been with anyone since Jake's death. And the fact that someone like Jonathan, so young and so attractive, could be interested in a thirty-five-year-old father was definitely flattering. "You could be right."

"Well, you big *perv*," Jonathan said, "you'd better pull that big, dangerous thing out of my body, because we both have to be up early and I'm exhausted from the flight."

Ed pulled out and loped down the hall to the bathroom. He removed the condom, cleaned up, and wet a clean white washcloth with warm, soapy water. When he brought the cloth back to the bedroom, Jonathan took it and wiped his flat torso clean. Then he got up on the bed and fluffed the pillows. He smoothed out the covers and tightened the sheets. And when everything was neat and orderly and perfect, he climbed into the bed and pulled the covers up to his chest. He smiled at Ed and patted the mattress. "Come to bed and put your arms around me. You must be tired, too, after the workout we just had."

Ed's head jerked back and he stood frozen. Evidently, Jonathan assumed he'd be spending the night with him. "Ah, well," Ed said, "Here's the thing. I thought you'd be going back to your hotel, is all." He didn't look him in the eye. He just stood there, with his penis hanging limp, rubbing his jaw with his right hand.

Jonathan hesitated for a moment, then tightened his lips and bolted from the bed. He crossed to the pile of clothes he'd left at the foot. He laughed and shook his head. "I'm sorry," he said, "I just assumed that…it's my mistake. I shouldn't have been so presumptuous. I'll leave right now so you can go to bed all alone tonight. Don't worry. I don't have to be told more than once when it's time to leave."

Ed took a deep breath and sighed. He sounded upset. "You're not mad or anything, are you?"

Jonathan moved fast. He pulled up his jeans and shoved his socks into his pockets. Then he slipped his bare feet into his shoes and said, "Of course not. Why should I be mad? You fuck me like you've just been released from prison, we have what I think is the best sex ever, and then you kick me out of your house. You're a real charmer, you are, Ed Richardson. I'm just the luckiest son-of-a-bitch in the world when it comes to men." He put his sport jacket on without his shirt; he rolled the shirt into a ball and shoved it under his arm.

"I didn't mean to get you upset," Ed said. He stood there in the middle of the room, with his arms spread out and a confused expression on his face. "I just thought it would be better if we keep things professional."

"You're right," Jonathan said. "Tomorrow we go back to being platonic again. We got this out of the way and we can move on." Then he reached into his pocket for his car keys and went to the door. He turned and said, "I'll see you in the morning. No need to walk me to the door."

Ed scratched his balls and sat down on the edge of the bed. He held his head in his hands and yawned. When he heard Jonathan's shoes clicking through the hall and down the stairs, he almost jumped up and ran after him. But he just sat there staring at a photo of Jake on his nightstand instead. He'd taken that photo right after Jake had come down from a hot air balloon ride. The front door slammed shut and a car out front screeched away from the curb. Ed smacked his forehead with the heel of his hand and sighed.

Chapter Five

While Ed's contractor forced a large screw into a kitchen cabinet, Jonathan smiled at the camera and said, "Join us next time to
see what happens with Dr. Ed Richardson's *Dream Away* kitchen.
You won't want to miss this."

He was baiting his viewers. There had been a slight problem
with the black granite counters Ed had chosen. It was nothing
serious, but he knew it was important to create a certain amount of
conflict for the show to be exciting. It was Friday and they'd been
filming for a week. So far, nothing had gone wrong. The contractors had shown up on time, all the materials had arrived in perfect
condition, and the entire kitchen had been gutted and was ready to
be rebuilt.

The camera shut down and the crew began to wrap up for the
day. Ed was in the living room sanding the wooden floor and Noah
sat on the center island in the kitchen watching Jonathan work.
Tucker rested beside his water bowl, waiting for his dinner. It was
almost six o'clock in the evening, and it had been a long week.

Jonathan smiled at Noah and asked, "How as school today,
buddy?" He looked too formal in his stuffy uniform. The gray
blazer and red tie stood out in the midst of the construction work-

ers. Jonathan always wore something casual during the construction process of the show so he'd blend in with the atmosphere. He was wearing jeans, work boots, and a red T-shirt that day.

Noah's brown oxfords swung back and forth. He stared at Jonathan and said, "It was okay."

"Just okay?" He didn't ask to be polite. He really wanted to know. In the past five days since he'd been working there, Jonathan had followed him around every day after school. He'd been curious about the cameras; he'd asked smart questions about how they edited all the clips. The better Jonathan got to know him, the more he liked him.

"It's school," he said, shrugging his shoulders. Then he jumped down from the counter and asked, "Hey, you wanna go to dinner with us tonight? My dad's taking us out later. We're going to pick Lisa up on the way."

Before Jonathan could answer, Ed said, "It's nothing fancy. Just a little place on Haight Street, a tapas bar. You're more than welcome to join us." He was leaning in the doorway, between the kitchen and the dining room, with his arms raised and his elbows against the door frame. He didn't know his shirt had risen and Jonathan could see his bare stomach. He was wearing loose painter jeans, and the elastic band from his boxer shorts was showing. The big fool had no idea how good he looked.

Jonathan smiled, then hesitated. The project was going well, but things were still a bit awkward between them. They treated each other too cautiously, as if the wrong word would ignite an explosion. He had a feeling Ed had been avoiding him all week, which was a good thing. After that last time they'd had sex, and Ed had asked him to leave, Jonathan had sworn to himself that if Ed Richardson so much as touched him with the tip of his finger, he'd set him straight.

"C'mon," Noah said. "You'll like the food. And Lisa's dying to meet you."

He didn't want to disappoint Noah and he was curious about Lisa, so he shrugged his shoulders and said, "I love a good tapas bar. I go to one in New York all the time with my boyfriend, Mike." This was the first time he'd mentioned he had a boyfriend. It was the first time he'd mentioned anything about his personal life.

Ed's eyebrows went up and his arms went down. He shoved his hands into his pockets and squared his shoulders. "I'll just go upstairs and clean up. Noah, you feed Tucker and walk him before we drop him off at the guest house." He didn't seem the least bit curious about the fact that Jonathan had a boyfriend.

"Can I go like this?" Jonathan asked. "Or should I change first?"

Ed looked him up and down fast. "Don't be ridiculous. You look fine. This place is very casual. I'm the one covered in saw-dust." Then he left the kitchen and upstairs to his bedroom.

Forty-five minutes later, Ed came downstairs wearing a clean white polo shirt, tan slacks, and brown shoes. There was a rust suede jacket over his arm. His dark blond hair was still damp and he smelled like shaving cream. This was the first time Jonathan had seen him wear something other than jeans and sneakers. He wanted to tell him he looked really good, but he didn't. Instead he said, "I think I should follow you guys in my own car."

Noah opened the front door and said, "You'd better come with us. Parking is hard there. My Dad can drop you off here later for your car." Then he hooked the leash to Tucker's collar and skipped out the door.

Jonathan waited to hear what Ed had to say about this, but Ed was busy looking for his car keys on a table in the hallway and he wasn't paying attention. So he put on his black leather jacket and followed Noah out to the car.

Even though November was one of the best weather months of the year in San Francisco, there was a chilly breeze that night. Jonathan was glad he'd worn a jacket because they had to walk a few blocks to the restaurant. The restaurant was crowded and small, but the food was excellent.

He loved Ed's best friend, Lisa. The minute she opened her mouth to speak and he heard her New York accent, a calm, familiar feeling settled over him. She was smart, beautiful, and had a sense of style that made her stand out in San Francisco. In the midst of so many women wearing baggy dresses down to their ankles and chunky Birkenstocks on their feet, she wore a black leather mini-skirt and pointy stilettos. And she didn't seem to care about fitting in with the others. Her blond hair was simple: long and straight and parted dead center. And you had to look closely to even guess she was in her mid-thirties.

When a woman in a baggy calico dress and gray hair down to her shoulders at the table next to them asked if the food was organic, Lisa rolled her eyes and gave Ed a look. Then she whispered across the table, mocking the woman to Ed, "No, it's not organic, you dumb and pretentious bitch...it's made out of plastic." They were sitting at a table for four, with Noah and Lisa on one side and Ed and Jonathan on the other. Lisa was directly across from Jonathan.

Noah laughed and Jonathan's eyebrows went up. Ed smiled and said, "You have to forgive Lisa. She goes into shock when she's out here. The woman sitting next to us is her worst nightmare: a classic, laid-back, San Francisco left-wing liberal who was most likely a hippie back in the sixties."

"Don't you like organic food?" Jonathan asked. What did he know? He'd never really thought much about it. There was a nice little grocery store in his neighborhood back in New York that had recently started carrying organic chicken. He'd tried some, but couldn't tell the difference.

Lisa smiled and smoothed out the napkin on her lap. Then she looked at the woman next to her and rolled her eyes again. "It's not that," she said, speaking with a hushed voice, "I'm all for eating chemical-free foods, but some people take it to the limit. Did you see the look on the poor waiter's face? I'd like to club her with an organic sausage, then wrap it around her throat."

Noah laughed again, and Jonathan cleared his throat. Noah seemed to be taking all this in his stride. He concentrated on his food, but didn't miss a word that was said.

"And don't get her started on politics," Ed said. "You'll never forgive yourself."

"Politics?" Jonathan asked. He'd never been a very political person. He voted in all the major elections, and usually it was for the person he thought cared the most about gay issues.

"Lisa is a die-hard Hillary Clinton supporter," Ed said. "You don't want to go there. She still hasn't forgiven the DNC for not nominating Hillary." Ed was smiling wide now, baiting Lisa to see how far he could go before she exploded into a political tirade.

"And please, whatever you do, don't mention the name Nancy Pelosi." Clearly, he was having fun with her and he wasn't getting into any serious political discussions.

But when Lisa heard him mention Nancy Pelosi, she clenched her fists and leaned forward. Then she hesitated, closed her eyes, and took a deep breath. She smiled and said, "Oh no you don't, you're not hooking me into a political discussion tonight. I don't discuss politics anymore. It's my new rule."

Then the conversation switched to Jonathan. Lisa wanted to know where he lived in New York, how long he'd been working in television and how he'd managed to land the job as host of *Dream Away*. He told her he'd always intended to be a journalist, but that he'd auditioned for *Dream Away* on a whim and somehow managed to get the job. He brushed it all off as pure luck and being in the right place at the right time. When he told her where his apartment was, it turned out that Lisa had a good friend who lived in his neighborhood.

Ed sat there staring at his dinner plate through all this, eating his food and listening to every word, glancing back and forth while they talked. His face was expressionless; he didn't raise an eyebrow or move his lips. But when she asked Jonathan if he had a partner or anyone special in New York, Ed's head went up and he almost dropped his fork.

"I'm involved with someone," Jonathan said. "His name is Mike and we've been seeing each other for more than a year. He's in England right now. He owns a public relations firm and he's working out of the London office for a few months." He lifted his hand and waved his new Movado watch in Ed's face. "He gave me this before he left." He wanted Ed to get a good look.

"Is it serious?" Lisa asked. She leaned forward and rested her elbows on the table. Evidently, Lisa loved to get all the juicy details.

Both Ed and Noah stopped eating and stared in his direction at the same time.

"He wanted me to quit my job and go to London with him," Jonathan said. "He's ready to settle down. He even wants to buy a place out in the Hamptons, move there eventually, and work mostly from home." He was looking at Lisa, but he was saying all this for Ed's benefit.

"My dad has a place in East Hampton," Noah said. He jumped into the conversation without thinking twice. He hadn't swallowed his food yet.

"Eat your dinner," Ed snapped, "and don't talk with your mouth full."

Noah swallowed hard and stared at his father.

"Well, that sounds pretty serious to me," Lisa said. "But you don't seem too excited about any of this." She also liked to analyze everything.

Jonathan shrugged his shoulders and smiled. "He's a great guy, and he'd do anything for me," he said. "What more could I want?" Then he lowered his eyes to his plate and started to eat. He certainly wasn't going into any details about his relationship with Mike in front of Ed. He'd already said enough. But out of the corner of his eye, he saw Lisa give Ed a look from across the table. Her eyebrows went up and she jerked her head in Jonathan's direction. Ed pretended to ignore her. He lifted his hand and asked the waiter if he could have another glass of wine.

Toward the end of their dinner, Ed took one last sip of his wine and spilled a few drops on his white polo shirt. Noah noticed it first and told him. Ed scolded him for pointing.

Lisa said, "You'd better ask the waiter for some club soda or you'll never get that out." They were waiting for the waiter to bring back Ed's credit card. Jonathan had offered to pay. He could have written it off as a business dinner with clients of the show. But Ed insisted, so he put his wallet back in his pants and shrugged.

"Salt is better than club soda," Jonathan said. "The salt will soak up most of the wine for the time being, and when you get home you'll have to pre-soak the stain with a mixture of hydrogen peroxide and a good, strong laundry detergent. Then wash it on a normal cycle and it should come out. But you have to do it right away."

They all stared at him for a moment. He felt as if there was a piece of food on the end of his nose. Lisa's head was tilted sideways, and Ed's eyebrows were up.

He shrugged. "I know how to do laundry," he said. "I like clean clothes."

"You'd better put salt on that right now, Ed," Lisa said. "Jonathan, you'd better do it for him. He'll just let it dry and we'll all have to look at that wine stain for the next ten years. And I'm no good with laundry. I send everything out." She reached for the salt and handed it to Jonathan.

"I'm fine," Ed said, waving his arm. "I'll just throw it into the washer when I get home."

But Lisa insisted. "Stop being so stubborn and let him at least put the salt on it."

Ed sighed and turned to face him.

Jonathan opened the salt shaker and placed it on the table. The stain was just below Ed's collar, on Jonathan's left. Lisa and Noah watched while he dipped a napkin into a glass of water and dabbed it lightly on the stain. From the way they stared, you'd have thought he was performing major surgery. He spread salt all over the wet section of the napkin and reached toward Ed's shirt. He didn't want to just dab it onto Ed's body; it would have fallen all over his lap. So he slipped his right hand through the opening of the shirt at the base of his neck, rested his knuckles on Ed's bare chest, and lifted the shirt so the salt wouldn't fall off. He gently rubbed the salt into the stain with his left hand, pressing against his right palm. Ed's chest was arm and solid and his chest muscle jumped a few times. When he inhaled, Ed's woody aftershave had mellowed to a soft, soothing aroma. Jonathan pinched his lips and focused hard on the stain, because when his knuckles touched Ed's chest something happened between his legs.

Ed sat still, staring up at the ceiling the entire time.

When Jonathan was finished, he patted it dry with another napkin and said, "Now when you get home, pre-soak with detergent and peroxide and put it through a normal cycle." He placed the napkin on the table and reached to get his jacket from the back of the chair. He had a full erection between his legs. It was a good thing he'd brought his jacket to cover his crotch.

After that, Ed drove Noah and Lisa back to the guest house. Noah wanted to show Jonathan his bedroom. Ed thought it was too late. He had to get up early; he wanted to finish sanding all the hardwood on the first floor that weekend. But when Jonathan saw Noah lower his head and pout, he said to the boy, "I'll come in for five minutes. But we can't stay long, because it really is past your bedtime."

The guest house was more like a small, one-story carriage house. When Tucker saw Jonathan walk through the front door, he raced to him with his tail wagging, jumped up, and licked his face.

There was a large living room/dining room section with an open concept kitchen at the end. Beyond that, there were two large bedrooms, each with its own bathroom. Noah's room was stark and modern with white carpet, a wall of tacky mirrored closets and a queen-sized bed. It was obvious this place had been pre-furnished with neutral things and that it was only temporary. The only signs that this room belonged to a little boy were a baseball bat and glove on a chair, a collection of superheroes on a desk, and a large poster of Barack Obama taped to the wall above the bed. When Jonathan commented on the poster, Noah smiled and said, "He's my ultimate hero."

But they didn't stay long. Ed stood near the door the entire time they were there, hands in his pockets, rocking on the balls of his feet. When Lisa offered to make coffee, Ed said he was tired and that Jonathan could come back another time. Lisa gave him a look, then asked Jonathan for his cell phone number. "I'm taking Noah shopping for new shoes tomorrow," she said, "I'm probably going shoe shopping myself afterwards. You're welcome to join us if you like, Jonathan."

Jonathan smiled. "I'd like that. I don't know anyone out here. Call me in the morning. I'll drive."

When Jonathan and Ed were back in the car, the ten-minute ride back to Ed's house was quiet. Jonathan mentioned how much he liked Lisa, and Ed smiled and nodded. Ed thanked him for putting salt on the wine stain, and he smiled and nodded. The click of the turn signal magnified. It felt as if they were driving cross country instead of a few miles. When they reached the driveway and Ed pulled up to the garage and switched off the headlights, the entire world seemed to go dark.

They sat there in silence for a moment, then Jonathan said, "Don't forget: hydrogen peroxide and detergent when you get into the house."

"Got it," Ed said.

"Then I guess I'll see you on Monday morning," Jonathan said. "Thanks for dinner tonight. It was fun."

But when he reached for the door handle, Ed grabbed his arm and pulled it back. Then he leaned over the center console and kissed him on the mouth. It wasn't a soft kiss either. He pressed his lips against Jonathan's, shoved his tongue inside his mouth, and tipped his head sideways. Jonathan grabbed the back of Ed's head with one hand and held his bicep with the other. The muscle bulged in his palm. His tongue was thick and warm; he smelled so damn good. And he tasted even better.

Jonathan wanted this man to control him. He wanted this hot hunk of sexy male flesh to pull him by the back of the head and throw him down again.

Ed stopped kissing for a moment and asked, "Should I stop? I will if you want me to." Then he ran his large hand up Jonathan's shirt and squeezed his right nipple. "I don't want to be presumptuous here."

Jonathan licked his ear and said, "Yes. We have to stop. We can't keep doing this." He knew it was wrong, and he'd already promised himself that he wasn't going to do it anymore.

Then Ed squeezed his nipple harder and kissed him again. "I really want to stop," Ed whispered into his ear, "but you look so good tonight. When you cleaned that wine stain on my shirt in the restaurant, my dick was ready to jump out of my pants. I never thought cleaning a wine stain could be sexy, but there you were."

Jonathan was surprised to hear that Ed had been just as turned on in the restaurant as he'd been. He'd seemed so stoic and reserved and unimpressed. He certainly knew how to hide his real feelings in public. "We should stop and I should go back to the hotel," Jonathan said.

But when Ed ran his strong hand down his stomach, he whispered, "You're so beautiful. I can't believe you'd even want to be with someone like me."

"I like you," Jonathan said, shrugging his shoulders. There were a few rough calluses now on Ed's palm from sanding the floors. He wanted to know what it was like to feel those calluses on his naked ass. So he unbuttoned his jeans, pulled down his zipper, and kicked off his shoes. His pants, his shirt, and his socks came off fast. When he was completely naked and ready to submit to all of Ed's needs, he wrapped his arms around Ed's wide shoulders and said, "Let's go in the back seat." Then he pulled a condom out of his jacket pocket and crawled to the back.

Ed followed him. His eyes were wide and his breathing was heavy. He sat down in the middle of the back seat, stretched his legs out, and pulled down his zipper. When his erection was sticking out of his pants, he covered it with the condom and held the base in his hand. Jonathan lifted his right leg over Ed's lap, faced the front of the car, and lowered his ass to the tip of Ed's dick. He spread his legs as wide as they would go and held the front seats for support. Ed inserted the tip into his tight hole. Jonathan closed his eyes and lowered his body. When Ed was all the way inside and he was sitting on Ed's lap rocking his hips in circles, he threw his head back, leaned into Ed's chest, and moaned.

Then Jonathan pressed the tips of his toes to the carpet and rode him this way for a few minutes. But it didn't take long for Ed to turn him all the way around so he was kneeling on the back seat and facing the rear of the car. Ed assumed total control and his penis never slipped out once. Jonathan spread his legs wide and Ed's hips began to buck. His dick went in and out fast. The car rocked and Jonathan's head went up and down. Each time Ed slammed his ass and went deep, Jonathan tightened his ass muscles and clamped down on Ed's penis.

It was desperate and rushed, just as it had always been with them. The windows fogged and the slaps against Jonathan's ass grew closer together. It was as if Ed couldn't get deep enough into his body. He held Jonathan's hips with such force and pressed so hard, he touched spots Jonathan didn't even know existed. They were sensitive, erogenous places that made his nipples hard. He hadn't been fucked in the back seat of a car since he was in college, and never with a man who made him feel as sexy as Ed did.

A few minutes later, Jonathan grabbed his dick and said, "I'm close. I'm really close."

Ed was fucking hard by then. He squeezed the sides of his ass and said, "Come for me. Jerk your dick for me."

Minutes later, while Ed hammered so hard his eyes rolled, he exploded all over the back of the seat. His prostate jumped and his toes curled. It was one of those rare, extended climaxes that left his balls tender with orgasmic sensations. A second after that, Ed grunted a couple of times and filled the condom. He bucked and pushed deep while his callused palms rubbed Jonathan's ass.

When it was over, he pulled his penis out of Jonathan's body and said, "Thank you for that."

Jonathan raised his eyebrows and pressed his lips together. Of all things, he hadn't expected a thank you from Ed. So he pulled him down to the seat and sat on his lap. Then he put his arms around his shoulders and kissed him on the lips. "You don't ever have to say thank you to me for having sex with you," he said. He kissed him again and said, "Now take off your shirt."

"Take off my shirt?"

"Yes," Jonathan said. "I'm going to pre-soak the stain and put it in the washing machine for you, because I know you're never going to do it yourself. And after that, I'm going to go back to my hotel and get some sleep." He lifted the shirt and pulled it over Ed's head.

"You don't want to spend the night?" Ed asked. There was a confused expression on his face.

Jonathan ran his fingertips up and down the back of his neck and said, "We both got what we wanted tonight."

"We did?"

Jonathan reached for the handle and opened the Range Rover's back door. Then he looked Ed in the eye and said, "I'd rather not talk about spending the night. Not after you kicked me out the last time we did this and I thought I was going to spend the night. We had a good time tonight. Let's not ruin it and get into a fight again."

Ed's eyes grew wide and he pressed his palm to his chest. "Ah well," he said. Then he looked at Jonathan's naked body and asked, "Aren't you going to put your clothes on to walk back to the house?"

He stepped out of the car and smiled. "There's no one home, and it's so dark no one can see me out here. I'll get dressed before I leave. Would you get my clothes in the front seat and bring them in for me?" Then he slowly went to the back door naked, with Ed's shirt pressed to his chest. There was huge smile on his face; he wiggled his hips on purpose. He didn't rush, because he knew Ed was staring at his ass the entire time.

Chapter Six

By the day before Thanksgiving, the old landscaping had been removed and new plantings had been professionally arranged. They'd worked fast to get it all in before Thanksgiving. Ed had decided to keep things simple: rows of neatly trimmed, round box-woods surrounded the house now, and a few of the original shrubs had been pruned and saved. He wanted to model everything after his house in East Hampton. The California landscaper hadn't been thrilled, but Jonathan had completely agreed.

Ed wasn't a huge fan of complicated flower gardens; he liked things to look uncluttered and in Yankee good taste. The house next door had rows of mums flanking the front walk, and he thought they looked like the buttons on a clown suit. The house across the street had too many palms and fruit trees; he thought they looked plastic and garish. Ed didn't even want garden orna-ments or statues. When the landscape designer cautiously suggest-ed two large urns for both sides of the front door to add texture, Ed agreed, with the stipulation that the urns would contain two more round boxwoods instead of flowers. Ed was determined to create a monochromatic look with a limited plant palette so the house would stand out above everything else in its setting.

And when the landscapers pulled away that day, he stood at the curb with his arms folded across his chest and smiled. The original architecture that had been hidden behind overgrown shrubbery for so many years shined in the afternoon sunlight. The terra cotta roof offered movement and dimension, and the white stucco walls added texture and light. The iron gate at the arched entrance that led to a small courtyard provided a focal point from the street. When he looked up at the round tower in the center of the house, it popped forward and anchored everything, connecting the north wing to the south wing with little effort.

And the new plantings were perfect. Each round boxwood was an exact replica of the one next to it, and the two in the urns beside the front door were slightly smaller in scale. For the first time since he'd moved to San Francisco, Ed finally felt like he was almost home.

But it wasn't all perfect. It was the day before Thanksgiving; his second Thanksgiving without Jake. And he was missing him so much his stomach ached. Since Jake had been gone, the same hollow feeling that invaded his entire body before all major holidays came back in full force.

To make things worse, he'd agreed to celebrate Thanksgiving with the two guys who owned the guest house where Lisa and Noah were staying during the construction. Lisa had become so friendly with them, she'd added them to her Facebook page and her Twitter account. She text-messaged them all the time and invited them for dinner once a week. Noah liked them, too. So Ed didn't have much of a choice. But if it had been up to him, he would have gone out to dinner, because the thought of spending Thanksgiving day with a happy gay couple only kept him awake longer each night.

Jonathan was a part of all this, too, and he'd been invited to Thanksgiving dinner with everyone else. He seemed to be everywhere; Noah never stopped mentioning his name. Jonathan and Lisa had become new best friends forever. They shopped together on weekends, took Noah on kid-friendly outings, and did power walks through the park with Tucker. When Noah came home and ran to tell Ed about their latest excursion, Ed smiled and listened closely. But he often felt disconnected and out of place. He knew he shouldn't feel this way. Whenever they went somewhere, they always asked if he wanted to go with them, but he'd shrug his shoulders and make up an excuse about finishing a project at the house. Sometimes Noah even begged him to come along. Jonathan would stand there with a raised eyebrow and his head tilted sideways, waiting for Ed's answer. When Ed said no, Noah's shoulders would sink into his chest and he'd shake his head and frown.

Ed couldn't figure Jonathan out for anything. He'd watch him closely while they shot film clips for the television show. When the camera was turned on, Jonathan didn't fake his smiles and he didn't raise his voice with an exaggerated lilt like some of the awful hosts he'd watched on home improvement shows. He didn't try to act and he didn't drop his sentences. With Jonathan, it was all natural and simple; he didn't even wear makeup. He talked to the camera and explained each step of the renovation as if he were talking to one person face to face. When there was a problem with something, he knew how to build the tension and conflict to keep his audience interested. He was young, handsome, and talented. He could have had any man—or woman; they loved him—he wanted. Not to even mention the fact that he had some guy, Mike, off in England who supposedly adored him. So why on Earth did he let Ed do the things he did to him?

It made no sense. Ed and Jonathan were together every day of the week, sometimes until very late at night. When the contractors were working and the crew was filming, they treated each other like virtual strangers. Ed would ask a banal question like, "Do you think you should get a clip of me sanding the door?" and Jonathan would nod and reply, "I think that would be good, Ed."

And when they were with Lisa and Noah, they behaved like distant friends who hadn't seen each other in years. They stood far apart, as if there was always an invisible person between them, and rarely looked each other in the eye. Noah even asked Ed once, "Don't you like Jonathan?" Ed had replied, "Of course I like Jonathan. He's great. Why would you ask me that?" Noah tilted his head and lowered his eyebrows. He said, "Because you always seem to be in a bad mood when he's around."

But Ed wasn't in a bad mood when he was alone with Jonathan, because the sex continued.

It was always fast and rushed and furtive, with heavy breathing and rapid heartbeats. Ed wanted to stop, but he couldn't control himself. And it often happened more than once in the same day, without a set pattern. There were days when Jonathan would arrive before the contractors and the crew. He'd say good morning to Ed, then fall to his knees, pull down Ed's zipper, and blow him on the back steps and finish him off with his hand. Later that same day, everyone would break for lunch and Jonathan would give him a look, then run his tongue across his bottom lip and Ed would be on top of him. He'd push him up against a door frame, pull down his pants, and nail him to the wall. They'd both climax fast, and Ed would put his dick away and Jonathan would pull up his pants and make believe nothing had happened. At the end of every single work day, when everyone went home, Ed would walk up behind Jonathan, pull down his pants again, and bang him over the kitchen counter for five minutes. Jonathan never said no. It reached a point where Ed always carried at least four or five lubricated condoms in his pocket just to be sure he was prepared.

On Thanksgiving, Ed got out of bed slowly. It was after eleven, and he'd been lying there staring at the ceiling since five. His leg muscles were sore because he'd fucked Jonathan in a weird position the night before. Jonathan had come back to the house to see the finished landscaping after dinner. It was well past nine, already dark outside. When he'd leaned over to get a closer look at the urns next to the front door, Ed put his hand down the back of his pants and shoved him into a small alcove at the front entrance. He pulled off all Jonathan's clothes and threw them over his shoulder down the front walk. When Jonathan was naked, he pulled down Ed's zipper and opened his pants. Then he put his arms around Ed's shoulders and jumped up and wrapped his legs around Ed's waist. Ed's short pants fell to the ground and he kicked them off his feet, then he pushed Jonathan against the front door and fucked him there. Jonathan locked his ankles together at the small of Ed's back and hung from his shoulders; they kissed and sucked tongues until they both climaxed. Then Jonathan kissed him goodbye, gathered his clothes, and drove back to the hotel naked.

Ed had experienced a wild climax that night—it made his knees tremble and his tongue fall from the side of his mouth. But it hadn't been easy. He'd had to bend his knees and rest his weight on his legs to keep his footing. Now the muscles in his shins were killing him. He'd never fucked anyone in that position, and he hadn't used those leg muscles in years.

He was tired that morning, too. There were dark circles under his eyes and he noticed a few lines at the corners. He'd only slept about two hours the previous night. He couldn't stop thinking about spending Thanksgiving with a gay couple who were practically strangers. This was one of those times he wished he hadn't rented his house in the Hamptons out for a whole year. They all could have flown back east for the weekend, and Ed could have visited Jake's grave.

After coffee, he filled the old tub with hot water and soaked for a long time. He usually took showers, but he figured the hot water would help his leg muscles. An hour later, he shaved and dressed. He pulled a white polo shirt and a pair of olive slacks from his closet. When he passed the table next to his bedroom door, he stared down at a small drawer containing a new box of condoms. He tilted his head and raised an eyebrow, then reached into the drawer and pulled a couple out of the box. He shoved them into his back pocket. He didn't think he'd need them, but with Jonathan around he couldn't be sure.

By the time he reached the guest house, it was almost three in the afternoon. They were supposed to go next door to the main house at three for an early dinner. He took a deep breath and parked behind Jonathan's rented car. It wasn't anything special; just a gray SUV with a bent California tag. But there was something about it that looked better than any other car on the road. And when he went into the house and saw Jonathan sitting in the middle of the living room floor playing a board game with Noah, he smiled for the first time that day.

Tucker barked and ran to greet him; Noah stopped playing the game and followed Tucker. While Noah hugged Ed and Tucker dancer around their legs, Jonathan stood up and smiled. He was wearing tight black pants and a white dress shirt. He crossed the living room, extended his right hand, and said, "Happy Thanksgiving, Ed."

Ed grabbed his hand and swallowed back hard. "You, too," he said.

Noah went back to his game, but Jonathan stood there staring at Ed's chest. He reached out and touched the left side of his shirt and asked, "Is this the same shirt with the wine stain?"

Ed's eyebrows went up and he looked down. "I think it is," he said. He hadn't thought about it when he'd pulled it from his closet.

Jonathan leaned forward and stared at the fabric. He pressed his face to Ed's body and took a deep breath. His hand was still on

Ed's chest. "It is the same shirt. I can still smell the fabric softener I used when I pre-soaked it."

A bedroom door at the back of the guest house slammed shut and Lisa called out, "I'm almost ready. I'll be there in a minute." She was never on time for anything.

Ed stepped back fast so she wouldn't see him standing there with Jonathan's hand on his chest. But more than that, his penis was growing. He *had* to step back or else his semi-erection would have become a full erection. If he'd been alone with Jonathan, he would have pulled down his pants and nailed him right on the living room floor.

When Lisa was finally ready, Noah filled Tucker's water bowl and they all went next door to the main house for dinner. It turned out to be a traditional Thanksgiving dinner and the hosts, Frank and Greg, were very gracious. They were attractive guys in their late thirties. Frank owned a prestigious design firm in San Francisco, and Greg was a producer at a local TV station. Their home was magnificent. From the marble entrance hall to the gilded faucets in the powder room, everything had been chosen with extreme care. Frank told Ed they'd traveled the world in search of merchandise for his high-end clients, then offered to help him with his renovation. Ed thanked him and politely declined. Ed wanted his place to look like a home, not a showplace. Frank and Greg shrugged their shoulders and didn't seem offended. But Ed thought he saw Jonathan stare down at his lap and smile when he told them he wasn't interested.

During dessert, when Frank asked Ed what he did for a living, Noah jumped in and said, "My dad's a veterinarian." He smiled and squared his shoulders, then said, "He had his own clinic back in New York and I used to help out after school."

Ed lowered his eyes and smiled. "Yes," he said. "I'm a vet." Whenever he talked about himself to strangers, he felt a pull in his stomach. How did he wind up here, in this strange city with these strange people? He looked up at the ceiling and thought, *Jake, what did you do to me*?

But then Jonathan asked, "Are you going to practice out here? Do you think you'll open another office?" He was holding a fork topped with a chunk of pumpkin pie, staring at Ed with furrowed eyebrows.

For a moment, Ed had a feeling Jonathan was about to smile. It sounded as if he knew an inside joke that no one else at the table knew. This was the first time Jonathan had ever asked about his future plans. "I'm not sure," Ed said, smoothing his napkin on his lap. He was staring at Jonathan, but talking to everyone. "I'm licensed to practice here. I took care of that ahead of time. But I haven't given it much thought. I think what I'd really like to do is open a non-profit free clinic for dogs and cats that need to get spayed and neutered. There's a real problem with overpopulation."

Jonathan's eyes grew wide and he tilted his head to the side fast. "I think that's absolutely wonderful." He looked into Ed's eyes, lifted his fork slowly, and placed the pumpkin pie inside his mouth. Then he licked his lips and started chewing.

"You do?" Ed asked.

Jonathan nodded yes. His mouth was full and his lips were moving.

Lisa and the other guys started talking about the benefits of rescuing a pet from a shelter, and Noah moved his fork around in circles as if he were playing with a toy airplane. But Ed couldn't take his eyes off Jonathan's mouth. He felt a tug between his legs and his penis started to grow. Jonathan chewed like he gave head: his lips puffed out and the sides of his face indented. Ed wanted to pull down his zipper and cover his dick with pumpkin pie so Jonathan could lick it all off with his tongue.

When it was finally time to leave, Ed thanked both Frank and Greg and promised to invite them to his first party when the house was finished. They seemed like nice enough guys, but Ed couldn't leave fast enough. He didn't like the way they'd slithered up to Jonathan all afternoon. Lisa and Noah wouldn't have noticed this, but Ed knew how to spot their kind from miles away. They'd paid

Jonathan extra compliments in a passive-aggressive way. Frank had asked him how often he worked out to keep such a fantastic body. Greg kept touching the skin on his arm, telling him it was so soft and smooth. Ed caught them both staring at Jonathan's ass more than once when no one was looking.

Oh, Ed knew what those two were up to. He and Jake had had a few gay friends who had been together as couples for years who'd done this sort of thing all the time. For some, it became a hobby. When they saw a good-looking young guy like Jonathan, it meant fresh meat, and their first instinct was to seduce him into a three-way.

So when Frank gave Greg a knowing look as they were all leaving and said, "Jonathan, would you like to stay for a while and watch a movie with us?" Ed stepped forward and said, "He can't. He has to call his boyfriend in England in about fifteen minutes."

It was none of his business what Jonathan did, but the words just popped out of his mouth.

"I do?" Jonathan said. His head jerked back and he stared at Ed with large eyes.

Everyone stared at Ed. So he laughed and said, "Maybe I made a mistake. I thought you mentioned earlier that you were calling Mike in England tonight." Ed wasn't even sure what time it was in England, but it was too late to stop now.

"Ah well," Jonathan said. "You're right. I almost forgot. I do have to call Mike. He's on a weird time schedule, and this is the only time I'll be able to get him for the next week." Then he lowered his eyebrows and stared at Ed with a confused expression.

"You have a boyfriend?" Frank asked. "I didn't know you had a boyfriend." He looked at his partner, Greg, and frowned.

"Oh yes," Noah said, "His name is Mike and he even gave him a mocambo watch."

"Movado," Jonathan said.

"Yeah, Movado," Noah said. He slipped out the front door and started running in circles. He made fists and pointed his index fingers as if he were shooting guns. A *pshew* sound came from his lips.

Lisa just stood there with her arms folded across her chest, waiting to see what Ed would say next.

"Well, thanks guys," Ed said, pushing Lisa out the front door, "But we have to get back for Tucker now. It's after eight and he's been all alone since this afternoon."

As they crossed down a walkway that led to the guest house at the end of the property, Frank and Greg both shouted, "Maybe we can do a rain check on the movie, Jonathan."

Jonathan looked back and smiled. "That sounds good, guys. Thanks again for a great Thanksgiving."

As it turned out, the lie about calling Mike in England came in handy when they walked Noah and Lisa back to the guest house. They brought them to the door and Ed said he had to leave. His excuse was he was getting up early to start sanding the second floor, because the film crew was shooting on Friday. And Jonathan said he really did have to get back to the hotel to call Mike. Lisa kissed them both goodnight, but she stared at Ed and pressed her lips together. Ed had a feeling she was catching on to them, so he stretched out his arms, yawned, and said, "I'm really exhausted and tomorrow is a busy day. But we'll all go out to dinner tomorrow night." Then he hugged and kissed Noah and walked back to his car.

Lisa smiled and said, "Sleep well."

He waved her off and smiled. "I'll try."

When Ed returned to his house, he sat in the driveway waiting. Sure enough, a few minutes later Jonathan's rented car pulled up behind him. They both got out at the same time. Jonathan crossed toward him and asked, "What's up with this phone call to Mike? I didn't know you cared about whether or not I called Mike."

Ed put his hands in his pockets and shrugged. "You knew I was lying and you still backed me up."

"I didn't want you to look bad," Jonathan said. "You didn't give me much of a choice. I just don't understand why you lied to them about me calling Mike."

"I did that for your own good," Ed said, leaning back against his car.

"And why is that?"

"Because those two only wanted to get you alone so they could get into your pants," Ed said. "I know what *they* were up to, and it wasn't about watching a movie."

"I'm not an idiot," Jonathan said. "I knew what they were up to all day, especially when Frank tried to put his hand down my pants in the kitchen while I was helping clear the table."

Ed clenched his fists. "He did that to you?" he said. "The guy is an asshole. It's a good thing I didn't see that."

Jonathan's eyes grew wide. "Give me some credit, Ed. I had no intention of watching a movie or doing anything else with them," he said. "And besides, even if I did, I don't see how it's any of your business. I don't ask anything from you. We aren't a couple. For all I care you can go back and watch a movie with them your- self if you'd like. I saw the way Frank kept staring at your crotch all day. I thought he was going to salt and pepper your dick and serve it up as a course."

Ed's mouth opened. "He was staring at my *crotch*?" Was Jonathan jealous?

"Like you didn't notice," Jonathan said. He folded his arms and stared down at his shoes. "You loved every minute of the attention."

Ed had no idea anyone had been staring at his crotch. He'd been too busy staring at the way Jonathan's ass looked in those tight black pants all day to notice. He spread out his arms and shrugged. "I swear this is news to me. I had no idea."

"Ah well," Jonathan said, "I guess I'd better go back to the hotel now and call Mike. His ears must be ringing tonight. At least then I can go to sleep tonight knowing I'm not a total liar."

As Jonathan turned to leave, Ed grabbed his arm and pulled him into his body. Then he held him at the small of the back with one hand, and the back of the head with the other, and kissed him on the mouth. Jonathan tried to pull back at first, but when Ed began to suck his tongue, he lifted his arms to Ed's shoulders and his young body went limp. Ed reached down between his legs and grabbed the bottom of his ass. "Let's go inside," he said.

When they were in the kitchen, Jonathan's pants and shoes came off first. Then he pulled off his shirt and said, "This time I want you naked, too."

Ed laughed. They usually went at it so fast there wasn't time for him to do anything more than pull down his zipper and whip his dick out of his pants. So while Jonathan got on top of the kitchen table and lifted his legs high in the air, Ed stripped down to nothing. He even pulled off his socks.

When he covered his penis with a lubed condom, Jonathan lifted his head from the table and said, "You look good naked. I really like that thin, sexy line of hair that runs down from your chest to your big, thick dick. You're a very sexy guy, even if you don't know it yourself. You remind me of a baseball jock."

"I like that," Ed said, "I used to play in college." Then Ed's dick jumped and he sucked his bottom lip in. He licked Jonathan's right ankle and said, "You make me look sexy. I'm just a jaded, thirty-five-year-old father when you're not around."

Jonathan lifted his legs higher and spread them as wide as they would go. "You're far from jaded, and I think you're just the right age. Besides, you look like you're still in your twenties, and you fuck like a horny teenager."

"You know how to make an older guy feel really good," Ed said.

"No one else but you," Jonathan said. "Did I tell you how much I like your hairy legs, and how I think those two little knobs on your knees are really hot? When I see you in short pants, I want to go down and kiss them."

Ed smiled. "No, you never told me that," he said. "But I'm glad you did."

Jonathan placed both his hands between his legs and pressed

down hard on his crotch with his fingertips. "I need you tonight," he said. "I need you really bad, Ed. Fuck me." Then his head rested on the table and he arched his back.

Ed took a deep breath and spread his hairy legs apart. He leaned back, grabbed his erection, and inserted the tip into Jonathan's soft hole. He was always amazed at how easily he could slip it into Jonathan's beautiful body. There were no awkward moments of pain; they never had to shift around to find the right position. If there was pain, Jonathan never complained once. This time the lights were on, so he could see the shaft of his penis slide all the way into Jonathan's gentle body. When it was all the way in and Ed's pubic hairs were pressed against the bottom of Jonathan's ass, he looked at Jonathan and asked, "Is that okay?" He knew Jonathan would tell him; they never hesitated to tell each other what they liked in bed.

Jonathan moaned, then rested his left ankle on Ed's shoulder and pressed his right foot against Ed's chest. He grabbed his own dick and said, "Hard, Ed. Do it hard like I know you like to do it to me."

Ed didn't waste time. His hips bucked fast and his balls slapped against Jonathan's ass. Jonathan held the side of the table with one hand so his body wouldn't move; he jerked his dick with the other. His legs hung over Ed's strong arms and dangled in limp circles.

When he went deep, Ed could feel Jonathan's hole clamp down on his dick. Jonathan had a powerful sense of control; he knew how to make his anal lips tighten and release at just the right moment.

A few minutes later, Ed climaxed first. He closed his eyes and threw his head back. His dick swelled, his balls jumped up in his scrotum, and he dropped a load into the condom. When he opened his eyes and looked down, Jonathan ejaculated a thick stream of white juice that flew over his chest and landed on his face. He'd tried to turn his head to avoid getting sprayed with his own come, but he hadn't been fast enough.

Ed pushed deeper and continued to fuck him with slow, easy bangs. Jonathan lifted his legs off Ed's arms and pressed his feet against Ed's chest. Then he looked up at Ed with wide brown eyes and licked his own come off his lips. When Jonathan swallowed back, Ed's mouth fell open.

Jonathan licked some more and smiled. "I like the taste," he said, shrugging his shoulders. "Hope it doesn't creep you out or anything."

Ed shook his head. "It's hot," he said. "Do it again."

When his face was clean and there wasn't a drop of come left, Ed finally pulled out and helped him sit up straight. He kissed him on the lips and turned sideways to remove the condom. While he was pulling it off, he felt Jonathan's hand reach down and grab his ass. He had gentle hands and his fingertips were soft. He squeezed it a few times and said, "Damn, you have an ass like granite. And it's small and cute."

Ed frowned. Jake used to say the same thing about his ass. And all of a sudden he felt overwhelmed. He wanted Jonathan to get dressed and leave. He'd been ready to ask Jonathan to spend the night, but when Jonathan started talking about his ass that way, images of his dead lover flashed before his eyes. "Will you be able to go out to dinner with us tomorrow night?" He didn't want to fight again. He was tired of fighting.

Jonathan jumped off the table and reached down for his clothes. He didn't even mention spending the night, which left Ed slightly confused. "Probably," Jonathan said, "I don't want to disappoint Noah." Then he reached down between Ed's legs and cupped Ed's penis and balls in the palm of his hand. Ed's balls overflowed in his palm. "I'll see you in the morning," he said. "Try to get some sleep tonight."

Ed's head jerked. When Jonathan grabbed his balls this way, a silky sensation passed through his entire body. "I'll try," he said. "But I can't promise anything. I just don't sleep much anymore."

He kissed Ed goodbye and left the house naked again, holding his clothes to his chest. On his way out the door, he turned to Ed and said, "By the way, I really like that idea about the free clinic for dogs and cats."

"You do?" Ed shook his head a few times. This was the last thing he'd expected to hear. He would have assumed Jonathan had forgotten all about the clinic.

Jonathan shrugged his shoulders. Then he looked at Ed's naked body and his head went up and down a few times. "I think a free clinic like that would be good for you, and for the entire community."

"I think so, too," Ed said.

When Jonathan turned to leave and stepped down the back stairs, Ed wanted to go after him and bring him back to spend the night. But he didn't. He just stood there with his hands on his hips, wondering why he couldn't move his feet.

Chapter Seven

The first weekend in December, Noah announced to everyone that he'd been chosen to perform in his school's Christmas show. It was a Saturday, and they were eating dinner in Chinatown. Jonathan wanted to take them all out, and this time he'd insisted on paying.

Noah made his announcement softly and slowly a few minutes after their meals had arrived. Ed and Lisa looked at each other, then at Noah. Jonathan congratulated him and reached for his chopsticks. But he noticed Noah wasn't smiling. He sat there staring at his food, with his hands folded on his lap and his head bent down.

Jonathan and Noah were sitting next to each other. He put his hand on Noah's shoulder and asked, "What's wrong, buddy?"

Noah shrugged his shoulders and continued to stare at his plate. "I think I made a really big mistake this time. I shouldn't have tried out. I'm not sure what I'm going to do."

"What kind of show is it, sweetie?" Lisa asked. She leaned forward with a set of chopsticks in her right hand.

"A regular Christmas show," Noah said. "I'm supposed to sing a solo." Then he looked at Ed and shrugged his shoulders. "It sounded like fun at the time. Remember, Dad, when Jake and me did that song and dance at my old school?"

Ed gave Lisa a look, then took a deep breath. "Ah well," he said. "You were both very good."

Noah folded his arms across his chest and sat back in his seat. "Yeah, but I couldn't have done it without Jake. He helped me rehearse the whole thing."

"I wish I could help you out," Ed said, "but you know that I can't even hum a song, let alone sing one." He looked at Lisa to see if she had any ideas.

She shrugged and said, "Maybe I can talk to Frank and Greg. I'll bet they could help you out, sweetie."

Jonathan put down his chopsticks and tilted his head in Noah's direction. "There's no need to get Frank and Greg involved," he said. "I'm sure I can get you through this, Noah."

Ed and Lisa looked at each other, then stared at Jonathan. "You can?" Lisa asked.

Jonathan looked at them and smiled. "Of course I can," he said. "I know how to play the piano, and I was a theater major my first two years in college before I switched to journalism." He fake-punched Noah in the shoulder and said, "Stop worrying and eat your dinner. We'll start working on your solo tomorrow on the piano in your Dad's living room, and you'll be great. I promise."

Noah lifted his head and smiled at Jonathan, then he looked at Ed and said, "We sure did get lucky this time, Dad." He sat forward and picked up his chopsticks. "Because I don't know what we'd do without Jonathan around."

Ed jerked his head and blinked. When he looked up, Jonathan smiled and shrugged his shoulders.

After dinner, Ed drove them back to the guest house, where Jonathan's rented car was parked in the driveway. When Jonathan pulled his keys out of his pocket, Lisa promised to drop Noah off at the house first thing Sunday morning so he and Jonathan could start working on the Christmas show. Then Jonathan kissed Lisa good night on the cheek and told her he'd talk to her in the morning.

When Lisa and Noah were inside the house, Jonathan looked at Ed and said, "I sure hope that piano is in tune, because if it's not, you'd better prepare yourself for some gruesome sounds tomorrow." He was walking backwards toward his car, noticing how sexy Ed looked that night.

Ed laughed. "I had it tuned the minute it arrived from New York," he said. "It's fine." He put his hands in his pockets and stared down at his shoes. "You can come back tonight and see for yourself if you like."

Jonathan knew he wasn't inviting him back for a sing-along

at the piano. They hadn't had sex since Wednesday. On Thursday there had been a problem with the new doors that led from the living room to an outdoor terrace. The contractor had ordered the wrong size and the old ones had already been removed. Ed had been livid, and he'd thrown a temper tantrum that day. The stress couldn't have been good for his blood pressure, but it did make for some interesting film clips for the TV show. Jonathan calmed him down and smoothed things over. The contractor wound up getting the correct doors late Thursday night and worked until after midnight to get them installed. And on Friday, they fixed the hole in the floor in the master bathroom, and didn't finish until seven o'clock in the evening. By that time, Noah and Lisa were waiting for them to go to the movies.

Jonathan smiled. Ed looked good that night. He was wearing baggy navy shorts and a cream-colored polo shirt. "I guess I could come back for a few minutes," he said. He had a secret gift for Ed in the back seat of his car. He'd ordered an unusual pair of underwear on the Internet that he thought looked really sexy and he was dying to see how Ed would look in them.

"You'd better not follow me, though," Ed said. "If Lisa or Noah is looking out the window, they might get the wrong idea."

When Ed said things like this, Jonathan wanted to kick him in the ass and go out drinking in a San Francisco bar filled with good-looking gay men. But he swallowed back and said, "I'll turn in the opposite direction and circle the block once."

A few minutes later, he pulled up behind Ed's Range Rover and clicked off the headlights. When he switched off the engine, Ed stepped out and walked to his door. Ed opened the door and Jonathan reached to the back seat for a brown paper bag and smiled. This was one of the little things Ed did that always gave him hope. Ed could have gone into the house and not waited for him. He didn't have to open the car door for him and walk him to the house. But he always did.

Jonathan got out of the car and handed Ed the bag. "This is for you," he said. "When we get inside, I want you to go upstairs and put them on. I'll wait for you in the bedroom."

Ed looked down at the bag and turned it back and forth. "What is it?"

Jonathan smiled. "It's a surprise." Then he lowered his voice to an almost-scolding tone and said, "And don't give me any arguments. Put them on and come into the bedroom so I can see them."

He was learning how to handle him. With Ed, you had to act fast and leave no room for explanation.

While Ed was in the bathroom putting on the underwear, Jonathan removed all his clothes and straightened out the covers on the bed. Evidently, Ed didn't like to make beds, but that didn't bother Jonathan. He was so excited about seeing Ed in the underwear, his penis was already erect. Before he got into bed, he turned the photo of Ed's deceased lover, Jake, in the other direction so he wouldn't be staring at them. He knew Jake would always be part of Ed's life, but that didn't mean his photo had to be there when they had sex. Then Jonathan went down across the width of the bed on his stomach and leaned forward on his elbows. He stared at the bathroom door and waited for Ed to come out. He was glad they'd fixed the hole in the bathroom floor Friday, because Ed would have had to go down the hall if they hadn't.

And that would have ruined his grand entrance.

When the bathroom door finally opened, Ed stepped into the bedroom and walked toward the bed. He was wearing a tight pair of gray long johns with buttons that ran from his neck down to his penis. But they weren't traditional long johns. This pair had short pants and no sleeves. You could see the muscles in his hairy legs pop and bulge; his biceps rounded and jerked. The fabric was a thin, elastic jersey that bunched up in his crotch and hugged his genitals. The outline of his thick penis rested to the left; he was still soft. He looked at Jonathan and his head went down. He didn't seem to know where to put his hands.

Jonathan stared at him and smiled. "You look so fucking hot," he said.

"I feel a little silly," Ed said, looking up and down his body. His arms were spread wide and his hands were open.

"Oh no," Jonathan said, staring at the soft bulge between his legs. "You look hot, man. I mean really hot." He patted the mattress and said, "Come here." He was still on his stomach, but his legs were spread wide now.

When Ed moved to the edge of the bed, Jonathan reached out and grabbed his crotch. Jonathan squeezed his balls with one hand and opened two of the underwear buttons with the other. The underwear opened wide and the flesh above Ed's pubic hair was exposed. Jonathan reached inside and pulled out his penis. He said, "Damn, you look so fucking hot like this." When Ed's penis was soft, it was thick and floppy; it dangled outside his underwear. Jonathan couldn't wait to slip the soft, spongy flesh into his mouth and suck it to a full erection.

Ed spread his legs and grabbed the top of Jonathan's head. "Suck it," he said. "Put those pretty lips around the head and take the whole thing to the back of your throat."

Jonathan smiled. He wanted Ed to talk dirty and give him orders. He wanted to please him and make him feel wonderful. Even if it was just for a short time. So he opened his mouth, stuck out his tongue, and gobbled it to the back of his throat.

Ed held the top of his head and pulled his hair, then started to buck his hips. He fucked Jonathan's mouth with gentle slams; his flaccid penis grew hard and hit the back of Jonathan's throat. Jonathan never once gagged or complained. He slurped and sucked until his face turned red and saliva ran down his chin; he could taste Ed's salty pre-come on his tongue.

Then Jonathan stopped sucking and got up on his knees. He kneeled on the mattress, arched his back, and unbuttoned Ed's underwear all the way. The tight gray fabric sprang back and exposed his solid, flat torso. This was the body of a real man, a man that made Jonathan's entire body weak with a desire he'd never known with anyone else. He ran his fingers up and down Ed's stomach and leaned forward so he could lick Ed's chest. He stuck his tongue all the way out and licked both chest muscles. When he was finished, he ducked his head and licked the rest of his torso.

Ed's penis was ready to burst. He grabbed the sides of Jonathan's face and said, "Get down on the bed, on your back, and lift up your legs."

When Jonathan went down, he spread his legs and lifted them up high. Ed reached into the nightstand for a condom, then got up on the bed and covered his erection fast. He grabbed Jonathan's left ankle and held his leg up high. He licked two fingers on his right hand next, and shoved them both all the way up Jonathan's hole at the same time. Jonathan closed his eyes. It was a blunt, forced sensation; his head went back and he moaned. This was the first time Ed had used his fingers. He'd been staring at Ed's thick fingers for weeks, wondering how they'd feel inside his body. And while Ed rolled his fingers around the inside of his hole, he begged, "Fuck me, Ed." He could see Ed's dick popping out of the gray underwear, and he just wanted him to shove it into his body and start slamming.

Ed pulled his fingers out and grabbed his erection. He inserted the head slowly and slid the shaft halfway into Jonathan's hole. When he leaned forward and started to buck his hips, Jonathan wrapped his legs around Ed's waist and grabbed his biceps. Ed's face turned red and he sucked his bottom lip in. Then he started to slam and pound Jonathan's ass with firm, swift thrusts. The bed rocked and the covers fell to the floor. Sweat dripped from his temples onto Jonathan's lips. His spicy underarm deodorant mixed with his own perspiration, creating a unique scent that filled Jonathan's head. It was stronger than usual that night. Jonathan had smelled it before when he'd least expected it. They be leaving a restaurant and Ed would lift his arm to pull out his wallet and Jonathan would catch a whiff. Or he'd be working on something in the house and lift his arm to grab something and Jonathan would smell it again. And each time it happened, he'd want to fall down on his knees and suck Ed's thick cock.

Ed fucked him for a long time that night without stopping or breaking the pace once. When he was ready to come, he slapped Jonathan's ass and said, "I'm close."

Jonathan grabbed his own dick and started jerking. "Me too," he said. "You go first." His legs were still wrapped around Ed's waist, and he still held Ed's bicep with his left hand.

Ed grunted a few times and scrunched his face. When his head went back, his eyes opened wide and he filled the condom.

And while Ed continued to buck his hips, Jonathan blasted a three-day load all over his own chest.

Jonathan tightened his legs around Ed's body and pulled him closer. "Stay inside for as long as you can," he said. "It feels like you're really part of me this way."

"Are you going to do it again?" Ed asked. He was rocking his hips in slow circles, still deep inside Jonathan's body. But he was staring at the come on Jonathan's chest.

Jonathan had to think for a moment. He wasn't sure what Ed was talking about. Then his eyes opened wide; he knew what Ed wanted. So he licked his fingers first and swallowed back. He stuck his tongue all the way out and licked slowly. Then he wiped his own come off his chest with the side of his hand and swallowed the rest. When he was finished, he said, "You really like that, don't you?"

Ed nodded, then said, "I'd like it even more if you were eating mine. So I think we should both get AIDS tests next week."

His eyebrows went up and he ran his fingers across the back of Ed's neck. He'd wanted to suggest this for a while, but he was afraid Ed would get weird and freak out on him. So he smiled and said, "I'll set up the appointments and we'll go together. I'm not promiscuous either. I'll be honest, without going into detail. I was sexually adventurous in college, but that was a long time ago and I've been tested since then and it was negative. But I agree that this is the right thing to do so we both know we're safe."

Ed leaned forward and kissed him. "I can't wait to see how it feels to get inside you without a condom."

He smiled. "And I can't wait to see how you taste. I've wanted to blow you and finish you off that way since we first met. But I know that's not safe."

Then Jonathan ran his tongue across his bottom lip and he felt Ed's cock jump inside his hole.

Chapter Eight

For the first time in more than a year, Dr. Ed Richardson slept straight through the night. It was one of those deep, unconscious sleeps that felt more like ten minutes instead of eight hours. He probably would have slept another three hours or even longer, but early that morning Jonathan reached between his legs and cupped his genitals in the palm of his hand. Ed was on his back, with his arms over his head. Jonathan's head was resting on his chest and one of his soft legs was hanging over Ed's thigh. He was squeezing Ed's balls with a light touch, rubbing his leg up and down Ed's hairy thigh.

At first, Ed spread his legs wider so Jonathan would continue to play with his balls. His toes curled and his penis started to grow in Jonathan's hand. But when he opened his eyes and saw the morning sun coming through the window, his head jerked to the right. He looked at the clock on the nightstand to see what time it was: seven in the morning. When he'd asked Jonathan to spend the night, he hadn't thought about Noah and Lisa coming over early that day.

Jonathan's head was moving down his body by then. He was licking a sensitive spot just above Ed's pubic hair, moving his lips down toward Ed's crotch. Jonathan arched his back and whispered, "I'm going to wake you up with a blow job, handsome, and finish you off with my hand." Then he started rolling his sweet tongue in circles around his pubic hair. He took long, deep breaths, pressing his nose to the base of Ed's dick.

But Ed bolted forward and jumped out of bed. His erection bounced against his thigh with a loud snap. He rubbed his eyes a few times and said, "We can't. You have to leave now."

Jonathan's head went up. He shook it a few times and said, "What?"

"Noah and Lisa will be here by eight," he said. "They can't find you here."

"Just tell them I came over early. They won't know I slept with you last night." He stretched his arms and yawned, still not understanding the magnitude of what Ed was telling him. Then he smiled and said, "I like the way that sounds…that I slept with you."

"They'll see your clothes," Ed said. His voice was fast and sharp. "Lisa will know, and I'm not ready for this. There's too much going on. I'm sorry. I'm really sorry, but you have to leave and come back."

Jonathan slapped the bed and sighed. "If it weren't for Noah," he said, "I'd probably leave and not come back today at all. First you ask me to spend the night, and now you kick me out first thing in the morning. It makes no sense, Ed. Most guys would just lie back and enjoy a good blow job. Are you ever going to be ready to move on with your life?" His voice sounded abrupt, as if he was really mad this time. "And I'm starting to wonder about myself now. What the *fuck* is wrong with me? Do I *enjoy* being insulted by you? I've never let anyone else treat me this shabbily, but I let you get away with it. I let you fuck me, then you kick me out and I smile and come back for more. Maybe *I'm* the one with the problem."

Ed ran his palm through his hair. He looked down at Jake's photo on the nightstand and saw it facing the wall. He knew Jonathan must have turned it around, and it dawned on him that this wasn't easy for Jonathan either. So he spread his arms wide and he raised his brows. "You don't have any problems, Jonathan," he said. "It's me. I need more time, is all. You're *perfect* just the way you are."

He meant it, too. He meant this with all his heart. "I'll make it up to you. I promise."

Jonathan shook his head and sighed. "You see, Ed," he said, "that's how you *always* get me, and I'm starting to think you know I can't resist it. You do something really shitty, like kick me out of your house like common trash, and then you say or do something really great and I have no choice but to forgive you. It's not fair. I have feelings, too."

Ed shrugged. He knew his reasons sounded more like lame excuses and irrational worries. But he wasn't ready to be part of a couple yet. "I'm sorry. I know you have feelings. I'm just not ready to get into this with Lisa, Noah, or anyone else. But most of all Noah. He lost a father last year and his entire world turned upside down in a matter of minutes. We went from being the perfect family with two gay fathers to being two lost souls. I don't think Noah has recovered from the shock. I need to keep his life as solid and stable as possible."

Jonathan looked him in the eye and said, "Ah well, since you put it that way, I'm okay with it. I don't want to confuse Noah either. I've really become attached to that kid. So I'll go back to the hotel, change my clothes, and come back to help him start rehearsing for the Christmas show."

Ed smiled. "You're the best. I'll make it up to you. I swear."

Then Jonathan rolled over on his back and rested his head on the edge of the bed. He reached down and grabbed his own erection and said, "We still have a few minutes, and you're still half hard from what I can see. We may as well get off before I leave. Come over here and I'll tea bag you while we both jerk off."

Ed looked down at his penis. It was almost hard, and he was still horny. Jonathan looked good, lying there naked in the middle of his bed with the sunlight across his thighs. "Really? You're not mad at me?" he asked. He wasn't sure he'd ever be able to understand why someone as young and talented and good looking as Jonathan would want to deal with someone his age, with so much extra baggage and peculiar habits.

"Yes, *really*," Jonathan said. "And yes, I am a little mad at you. But I understand. Now grab your dick and get over here, unless you'd rather I didn't swallow both of your balls into my mouth and suck them while you jerk off."

Ed's eyes widened and he stepped toward the bed. When he bent his legs and dropped his balls into Jonathan's open mouth, he couldn't think of anything else he'd rather do.

* * * *

The baby grand piano in the living room had been covered with tarps for weeks because of all the construction on the first floor. But now that the kitchen was finished and the floors had all been sanded and refinished, there was no need to keep it covered anymore. The walls hadn't been painted yet, but Ed could always put a sheet over the piano. Ed had decided to paint all the walls in the house bright white to complement all the rich walnut doors and trim. He'd collected a great deal of art over the years; his taste leaned toward Andrew Wyeth's works, and the style of the Hudson River School. But he had a few abstracts, too. One of his favorites, a large modern dated 1971, was by a New York artist named Neil Loeb. Ed decided on white walls, because didn't want any garish colors fighting with good paintings. He also wanted to keep things simple and monochromatic.

When he pulled the tarps off the piano, he decided to polish it with Butchers Wax. And by the time he was finished, Noah and Lisa stormed through the back door, screaming his name. They were late. It was after eight thirty. Tucker was with them. He ran to Ed first, wagging his tail, then did a full inspection of the house. He sniffed every viable surface, taking in the scents of the camera crew and the construction workers, trying to find out what he'd been missing over at the guest house.

A few minutes after that, Jonathan knocked on the back door and stepped into the kitchen. His dark brown hair was still damp from the shower, and he was wearing a light green V-neck T-shirt and baggy tan cargo pants. He was carrying a box of doughnuts from a small bakery not far from the house, and two white grocery bags from a gourmet store on the other side of town. Ed was helping Lisa make coffee and Noah was in the living room placing his music sheets on the piano. Tucker ran to Jonathan first. He jumped up and licked his face. He got so excited when he saw him, he actually had a small choking attack.

Jonathan lifted his arms so Tucker wouldn't get the food, and

Ed shouted, "Down, Tucker." Then Ed ran to Jonathan and took the box and the bags from his hands. "Leave him alone," he scolded the dog. "You just saw him last night."

Lisa said, "I don't blame Tucker. When I see Jonathan, I want to wag my tail and lick him too." She put down a bag of coffee and ran over to kiss him on the cheek.

Ed felt an unusual pang of jealousy. He knew she wasn't serious, but it made his stomach jump. He smiled at Lisa and said, "Sounds like you need a date. How long has it been?"

"How long has it been for *you*?" she shot back.

Ed wasn't sure whether she was testing him about Jonathan or not. She had excellent intuition, and when she suspected a romance, she was usually right. So he backed down and said, "We're probably even."

Jonathan stood there in the doorway, rocking on the balls of his feet, looking awkward. He put his hands in his pockets and said, "I wasn't sure what to buy, so I bought a little bit of everything. There are doughnuts, muffins and bagels. And I stopped and picked up some cream and sugar for coffee and a few other things, like jam and butter and cream cheese. I picked up some juice and milk and cereal, too. I figured the refrigerator was empty, and there are *two* growing boys in this house."

Lisa pulled a container of milk from the bag. She laughed and said, "You're finally starting to figure Ed out," she said. "He's just a big boy."

Ed ignored Lisa. He stared at Jonathan and said, "Well, thank you. I actually do like a glass of milk in the morning. I haven't had it for a while." He didn't mention this aloud, but it made him think about Jake. Jake had always made sure there was fresh milk in the house even though he'd never touched it himself.

Lisa smiled, then gave Ed a look. "The refrigerator is always empty around here. Ed hates going to the grocery store. It freaks him out."

Ed shrugged his shoulders. "It doesn't freak me out. I just hate those places, and I hate waiting in line. But I know how to manage and Noah will never go hungry as long as I know how to order from a menu." Jake had always been the one who did all the grocery shopping, and after he'd died, Ed had to figure out how to do it alone. Ed looked at Lisa and said, "Besides, when was the last time you used your oven?" She was just as bad as he was when it came to keeping a kitchen well stocked. In the past year, Noah had eaten at all the best restaurants in town, but the only home-cooked meal he'd had was Thanksgiving dinner at Frank and Greg's.

Lisa pulled out a container of whipped cream cheese and smiled. "I guess we're both pretty bad when it comes to domestic things." She shook her head and said, "Poor Noah. He'll wind up marrying the first woman who bakes him a pie."

When Noah crossed through the kitchen door and saw Lisa pulling all the food out of the bags and placing them on the black granite countertop, he said, "Dad, look. It's real food. I'm starved." He ran to the cereal box and lifted it from the counter. His eyes glazed over and he sucked in his bottom lip. Then he turned to Jonathan and said, "This is my favorite cereal. My dad used to buy it all the time back in New York."

He was talking about Jake, not Ed.

"It was just a lucky guess," Jonathan said.

Ed put his hands on his hips and shook his head. "I'll go to the garage to locate some bowls and dishes and some silverware," he said.

All they had were mugs. The kitchen remodel was finished, but he hadn't had time to put everything back where it belonged. It still looked and felt more like a showroom than a real kitchen. On his way out, he turned toward Jonathan and said, "Unless you brought those, too." He was being sarcastic on purpose. Everything Jonathan did always came out so damn perfect. If Ed could have found at least one flaw in him, it would have made things so much easier.

"Sorry," Jonathan said, "the market was all out of bowls and spoons this morning. But I'll go out to the garage and help you with the boxes if you like. A man your age shouldn't be lifting anything too heavy."

Lisa poured coffee into a mug and smiled. "I like that, Jonathan," she said, "You can be a real smart ass when you want to be."

Ed scratched the top of his head and smiled even wider. Evidently, Jonathan could be just as sarcastic as Ed could be, and he wanted Ed to know it. "No. I'll be fine. The old man can still manage."

But Jonathan wasn't finished with him yet. On his way out to the garage, Jonathan shouted, "Did you sleep okay last night, Ed?"

Ed stopped and turned back to face him. His eyes narrowed and focused directly on Jonathan's eyes. He folded his arms across his chest and said, "Never better. I actually slept through the entire night for the first time in over a year."

Lisa and Noah looked at each other; they knew he hadn't slept a full night since before Jake had been killed. Noah smiled and said, "Maybe it was all that Chinese food we had last night, Dad. We should go there again tonight. I slept good too."

"*Well*, Noah," Ed said, "You slept *well*, not good." He was still staring into Jonathan's eyes.

Noah wasn't paying attention. He'd opened the cereal box and he was digging inside for a handful.

"Was it the Chinese food?" Jonathan asked.

Ed shrugged his shoulders and smiled. "It could have been, but I'm not totally sure yet."

Chapter Nine

While Jonathan and Noah rehearsed his song for the school Christmas show, Ed painted the upstairs hallway white. It was Saturday morning, December twentieth, three days before the show. Jonathan had been playing the same song for two hours without stopping longer than five minutes. And Noah had been singing. He was good student, and he sang well for a ten-year-old. He lifted his head high, took deep breaths through his diaphragm, and opened his mouth wide so the lyrics wouldn't sound muffled.

Ed came jogging down the stairs wearing the baggy camouflage shorts he'd worn the first time Jonathan had met him. He had a paintbrush in one hand, a roller in the other, and there were white paint spatters across his right cheek. He looked cute, Jonathan thought. He'd been laboring all week on the house along with the other workers because he wanted to celebrate Christmas Day there. The second floor was still a mess and the bathrooms weren't finished. But the first floor was ready to at least host Christmas dinner. Most of the furniture and art was still in storage, but the kitchen was ready, the floors were finished, and the walls had been painted.

Ed's new dining room furniture had been delivered Friday

afternoon. It was a heavy, dark Jacobean table that sat fourteen people comfortably, with large hand-carved chairs upholstered in antique Spanish tapestry. Ed had originally wanted a modern glass table, then changed his mind when Jonathan showed him a photo in *Architectural Digest* of a celebrity home in the Hollywood Hills just like his with a more traditional look.

As he passed through to the kitchen, Ed shouted, "I'm going to clean up now, and we'll leave in a few minutes, Noah."

"Okay, Dad," Noah said. He turned to Jonathan and asked, "How was I? Do you think I'm ready for the show?" His eyebrows were furrowed and his lips pinched together.

"You were great," Jonathan said. "I think we've rehearsed enough for today. You get Tucker's leash and take him out so you'll be ready by the time your dad is cleaned up."

They were going out to buy a Christmas tree that afternoon, and Jonathan and Lisa were going Christmas shopping and stopping at the airport to pick up Jonathan's friend, Joel. Joel was passing through San Francisco on his way to a business trip in the Orient. He was only staying over one night, and he'd made plans to take Jonathan out to dinner.

"Can we practice again tomorrow?" Noah asked.

"Of course," Jonathan said. "We'll go over this song every day after school this week until the day of the show." Then he stood from the piano and patted him on the back. "So stop worrying. You're gonna be great."

Noah smiled and slapped his thigh a couple of times. Tucker stood up and crossed to the piano. "C'mon, boy," he said to the dog. "We're going out for a walk, and then we're going to get a Christmas tree."

When Noah said they were going out, Tucker got so excited and wagged his tail so hard, his entire hindquarters moved back and forth.

Noah hooked his leash to his collar and walked to the back of the house. Then Jonathan went into the kitchen, where Ed was washing his hands and his arms with dishwashing detergent and a kitchen towel. Jonathan frowned when he saw the water splashes all over the granite counter, and he shook his head when he saw Ed wiping paint from his hands with a good dish towel. "I probably would have used the powder room," he said. "It's more sanitary. And that dishwashing detergent is too harsh for your hands."

Ed shrugged his shoulders and rubbed a splotch of white paint from his wrist. "It's all the same," he said, "A sink is a sink. Soap is soap. Besides, I hate to mess up the powder room. It looks so good."

Jonathan smiled and crossed to the kitchen sink. Ed was probably right. He would have messed the entire powder room up with splashes and paint. And it was one of Jonathan's favorite rooms in the house. Ed had decided on black marble, from floor to ceiling, with a black pedestal sink, a black toilet, and rock crystal wall sconces dripping in gilt. The finished result looked like a jewel box. He took the wet dish towel from Ed's hand and said, "Here, stand still." Then he gently rubbed the white paint off Ed's cheek.

"I didn't know I had paint on my face," Ed said.

His strokes were gentle, as if he were rubbing paint off Ed's penis. He did it on purpose for two reasons: he didn't want to hurt his skin, and he wanted to see if he could get him aroused this way.

Without turning his head, Ed's eyes moved to the right so he could look out the window. Noah was in the back yard with Tucker running in circles, so Ed reached down and grabbed Jonathan's ass. He squeezed it a few times and said, "If you keep rubbing my face this way, my dick is going to pop out of my pants."

Jonathan smiled and grabbed his erection through the fabric of his shorts. He continued to rub his cheek, spreading his legs wider so Ed could get a good grip on his left ass cheek. Ed's large hands were still sopping wet. Jonathan was wearing light olive slacks and he hoped there wouldn't be a wet handprint on his ass. "You should be tired by now," Jonathan said. "You painted all morning, and before that you gave me a real workout. My legs are actually sore right now."

Jonathan had arrived early that morning. The minute he'd walked through the door Ed had kissed him, pulled down his pants and fucked him over the piano bench. They'd both been tested for HIV/AIDS by then, and both tests had returned negative. And now that Ed knew he could fuck him raw without worrying, he took advantage of every opportunity.

"You didn't complain while I was doing it to you," Ed said, squeezing his ass tighter. "I would have stopped if you'd asked." His voice was low and deep. "Besides, I wanted to give you something to think about when you're with this friend of yours later today. This so-called *straight* guy who you had sex with in college."

Jonathan had told him almost everything about Joel, from the casual sex they'd shared in the dorms to the fact that they'd always remained good friends. "He *is* straight," Jonathan said. "He's been married so many times I lost track. And I can't even keep up with the list of women he dates. Trust me, Joel likes pussy. He's a pussy *hound*."

Ed grabbed his ass and pressed his middle finger into the center. "I'll bet he liked this, too."

"He did," Jonathan said, "but that hasn't happened in years, and it's not going to ever happen again. So let's just stop talking about it. Joel is nothing more than a very good friend now." He was beginning to wonder about whether or not he should have mentioned anything about his past with Joel. He could have said they'd just been college buddies and left it at that. He didn't tell Ed all the details about his own sex life in college, and how he'd taken on groups of drunken football players. He wasn't ashamed of his past; he'd enjoyed the men he'd been with. But some details about the past were not meant to be discussed, and he wouldn't have asked Ed to discuss his past sex life in detail either. He didn't want to know.

"Is Joel good looking?" Ed asked.

The paint was off his face, but Jonathan continued to rub with gentle strokes. He leaned forward and kissed him on the mouth. It was a soft, wet kiss; his lips puffed out and touched him lightly. He didn't want to talk about Joel anymore. When he inserted his tongue and pressed it against Ed's he closed his eyes and took a deep breath.

No man—not Joel or anyone else—had ever been able to make him feel the way Ed made him feel.

Then the front door slammed shut and Lisa shouted, "Is anyone home?"

Jonathan stepped back fast and Ed turned to the sink. Ed leaned forward and pressed his body against the cabinet and said, "We're in the kitchen." He had to hide his erection. He wasn't wearing underwear and he'd pitched a full tent in the camouflage shorts.

But fifteen minutes later, when Jonathan was driving the two of them in the SUV to Market Street, Lisa said, "I noticed something strange back at the house. Maybe I shouldn't mention it, but I'm curious."

Jonathan was driving, and they were heading over to The Flat Iron Building so he could order Sees Candies and have them sent as Christmas gifts to friends back in New York. "What did you notice?" he asked. Had she seen Ed's erection? Maybe she'd seen them kissing. He felt a lump in his throat and he swallowed back hard. *He* didn't care if she knew, but Ed would be furious.

She adjusted her seat belt and turned to face him. "Well," she said, "when we were walking out of the kitchen, I saw a wet handprint on the back of your pants. And Ed was standing there with wet hands. I was just wondering how you got a wet handprint on the middle of your butt." She sounded casual and relaxed, but she was leaning forward on the edge of the seat, with her elbow on the center console and her chin in her palm.

Jonathan smiled. "Would you believe me if I said I backed into Ed's hand by mistake?"

She shook her head and said, "No."

"Would you believe me if I said that Ed was trying to kill a bug and he slapped me there without thinking first?" He gave her an innocent look and added, "A really big bug."

"Ah no, I wouldn't. I'm not a fucking idiot, Jonathan."

He clicked the turn signal and pulled to the side of the road. Then he looked her in the eyes and asked, "What would you believe?"

"C'mon, Jonathan," she said. "Give me some credit. I'm a woman. I've seen the way you two look at each other. At first I thought I was reading too much into it, but last week I stopped by the house on my way to pick Noah up from school and I saw Ed nailing you to the garage wall. I ran back to the car so fast, I almost broke a heel."

Jonathan squinted and made a face. He thought he'd heard a car door slam that afternoon, but he and Ed had just found out about the AIDS tests and Ed had been so eager to get into his pants that Jonathan could barely concentrate on anything else around them. Ed had practically grabbed him by the collar and dragged him out to the garage, and all he'd wanted to do was spread his legs and close his eyes. Ed had been planning this—he had lube in his pocket and a full erection between his legs. He'd pushed him up against the garage wall, yanked down his pants, and shoved his erection into his body so fast Jonathan thought he'd lost his hearing. It had been their first time without a condom, and it was just as romantic for Jonathan as if he'd thrown him down on a bed of roses. Ed had filled him with such a full load he'd had to go back to the hotel to shower and change his pants afterward.

Lisa smiled. "So, what's going on?"

He sighed. "I'm not totally sure," he said. What else could he say? He wasn't going to get into the details about how they'd been screwing around since the first day they'd met, or how many times they did it on any given day. So he smiled and placed his hands on his lap. "We're fond of each other."

She pushed his shoulder and laughed. "You're *fond* of each other? Ed drools when you walk by, and you stare at him as if he's a Greek god, and you call that 'fond'?"

Jonathan pressed his lips together and thought for a moment, then he faced her and said, "We really don't know what we're doing. Seriously. Ed isn't ready for a commitment, and I still have Mike back in New York."

"Give me a break," she said. Her New York accent grew stronger and she pointed her finger in his face. "Don't pay attention to what Ed says he's ready for or what he's not ready for. I love him, but sometimes he can be a real idiot. I've known him for a long time, and I knew how happy he was with Jake. I also saw his life crumble when Jake was killed. But since you've been around, it's like a huge void has been filled again. He's almost back to normal. I feel like I've finally got my best friend back and I don't want to lose him again."

Then she softened her voice and reached out for Jonathan's hand. "And, frankly, from what I saw last week in the garage when Ed had you pinned to the wall, he's filling a huge void in *your* life, too."

Jonathan's eyebrows went up and he blushed. "I can't believe you just said that. That's just wrong." But she was right. Ed was filling a void in his life he never thought could be completely filled, and he wasn't thinking about sex.

She shrugged. "Does Mike make you feel like Ed makes you feel? Because whenever you talk about Mike, which isn't often, I don't even see a sparkle in your eyes."

He sighed again. He didn't want to discuss Mike. "Do me a favor, Lisa? Don't let Ed know we talked about this. It would freak him out. And he's really worried about Noah. He wants to keep his life stable."

She laughed and waved her hand. "Don't worry about me. I know how to handle Ed. And as far as Noah is concerned, you've been the best thing for him, too."

After that, they went shopping. They parked and set off in opposite directions because they both had long lists and wanted to do as much shopping that afternoon as possible. Jonathan was spending Christmas in San Francisco. When Noah found out the only family Jonathan had left back East were cousins in upstate New York, he practically begged him to stay and spend Christmas with them. So he had to shop for Noah, Lisa, and Ed. On top of that, he had to buy something for each crew member and a few of the other people he'd met in San Francisco. When they finally met up again late that afternoon, he and Lisa filled the back of his SUV with so many bags and packages, he could barely see out the back window. He had to get out and move some of them to the back seat.

When they were in the car, Lisa said, "I'm exhausted. Did you get everything you need?"

"I think so," he said, starting the car, "I'll go over my list later, but I think I'm finished. And I was really good, too. There was this first edition of *How the Grinch Stole Christmas* in Gumps, and I didn't buy it for myself."

"Why not?"

"It was too expensive and too self-indulgent even for me," he said. "And trust me, I know how to spend money."

He'd spent more money on Ed than he'd planned to spend. He bought him an expensive black leather sport jacket and a bottle of sexy, spicy cologne. And in a small box, hidden beneath a sweater he'd bought for Lisa, there was another gift for Ed: a sex toy he'd found in an erotic boutique that he hadn't been able to resist. He would give *that* gift to Ed when no one was around, and he would wait to see the expression on Ed's face when he opened the box.

When they drove to the airport, Joel was already waiting outside the terminal with his bags. He was wearing a black jacket, a white T-shirt, and low-rise jeans. His face was tan and his blond hair was windblown. He looked more like he'd just come off a cruise ship than an airplane. Jonathan pointed and said, "There he is."

Lisa's mouth fell open and she said, "That's Joel? The college friend with all the money?"

"Yes."

"You never said he was so damn hot, Jonathan," she said. "The guy is gorgeous."

Lisa didn't know anything about Jonathan's past sexual experiences with Joel. She knew he'd been married and divorced a few times, that he traveled extensively for work, and that he was based in New York. "I never think of him that way," he said, "but you're right. He is gorgeous."

He pulled up to the curb and got out to help him with his bags. Joel gave him a tight hug and looked over his shoulder. When he saw Lisa sitting in the front seat, he asked. "Who's that in the car?"

Jonathan stepped back and said, "It's my friend, Lisa. She's Ed's best friend. Ed is the guy who owns the house where we're filming the show. Lisa is from New York, and she's out here helping Ed with his son while the house is being renovated."

Joel smiled. "Well, then," he said, "let's go meet Lisa." Then he rubbed his hands together, smiled, and went to her window without waiting for Jonathan to make a formal introduction. When it came to attractive women, Joel had never been shy.

While Joel smiled and flirted with Lisa, Jonathan tried to arrange his bags in the back seat. But they were so large there wasn't any room for Joel to sit down. When Jonathan mentioned the problem, Lisa turned and said, "I guess that means we'll all have to sit up front, then. I don't mind sharing my seat for a few minutes."

Joel opened the passenger door and said, "That's fine with me."

Jonathan looked up at the sky and shook his head, then he closed the back door and crossed back to the driver's side so he could take Joel to his hotel.

Chapter Ten

They put up the Christmas tree at the far end of the living room, beside the piano in front of a window that faced the street. Tucker wouldn't stop sniffing it. The poor thing could never seem to understand why they brought a real tree into the house every year. It was nine feet tall and Ed had to secure it to the window sill with an eye hook and a thin cord to keep it from toppling over. He carried in boxes of ornaments and lights from the garage that they had been accumulating for the past ten years. It was amazing that despite the cross-country move, they were all still in perfect condition. Even the thin crystal icicles were intact, because Jake had packed them all so carefully the last time he'd taken the Christmas tree down.

But Ed wasn't sure about the location of the tree. He tried to convince Noah that the tree would look better to the right of the fireplace, but Noah flatly insisted on placing it near the piano. Noah tightened his face and pointed to the end of the piano. "Dad always put it next to the piano, and that's the best place for it."

Ed ran his fingers through his hair and smiled. "Then that's where we'll put it this year," he said. Ed had never paid attention to these details when Jake had been alive. He'd spent six days a week at his animal clinic in New York, and Jake had been the one to put up the Christmas tree, organize the holiday meal, and handle the decorations. Now all these things kept cropping up, and Ed wasn't always sure how he was supposed to deal with them. This was the first tree Ed and Noah put up without Jake. The first Christmas after Jake's death, Ed had booked a trip to Hawaii and they'd spent the holiday in a tropical paradise, trying to forget how devastated they were.

By the time Jonathan and Lisa returned from the stores, the tree was decorated and Ed was ready to plug in the lights. Lisa and Jonathan came into the room and stared at the tree. Their arms were filled with packages. When they saw the decorations, they both smiled and told Noah it looked gorgeous. Then Ed plugged the cord into the wall and thousands of multicolored lights illuminated the ornaments. There was silver and gold glitter on Noah's face, and Tucker was chewing on a wrinkled red ribbon.

Jonathan placed his packages on the floor looked the tree up and down. He'd been the only child of elderly parents, and he'd lost them both within a two-year time frame in his early twenties. He hadn't bothered with a Christmas tree in five years. "I really like the colored lights," he said. "They make the tree look warmer than all white lights." Then he patted Tucker on top of the head a few times and pulled the ribbon from his mouth. The dog inspected the bags and wagged his tail.

Noah looked at Ed and nodded. Then he told Jonathan, "My other dad, the one who died, always liked them better, too."

Jonathan put his hands in his pockets smiled. "You did a great job, buddy. And I've never seen so many ornaments. It must have taken all afternoon to decorate."

Noah lifted his head and squared his shoulders. "My dad used to collect them. He bought new ones every year. There are so many we can't put them all on the tree." Then he pointed to a small orna-ment in the middle of the tree—a blown-glass multicolored hot air balloon. It was very detailed, with two small delicate people stand-ing in the basket, waving their arms to an invisible crowd below them.

Noah smiled and said, "This one was his favorite. He loved hot air balloons." Then he stared at the ornament and sighed.

Ed cleared his throat and said, "We'd better start getting ready for dinner now." He knew the fact that Noah could talk about Jake this way was a good thing, and it meant that Noah was accepting Jake's death. But Ed didn't want to talk about it for too long.

Lisa put her bags down and said, "It looks great, Noah. You guys did a fantastic job today." Then she turned to Ed and asked, "Is it okay if we keep everything we bought over here in the base-ment? The guest house has no storage, and it's silly for Jonathan to keep his things in a hotel room."

"Sure," Ed said. "I'll carry them down for you." He was dying to ask about Jonathan's college friend, but he didn't want Lisa to get the wrong idea.

"Oh no," Jonathan said. "I'll carry them down. There are things we don't want *you* to see."

Ed felt a tug in his stomach. He hadn't thought about shopping for the holidays. With all the renovations and working so hard to get the house together for Christmas,, he'd totally forgotten to go shopping. He'd have to sneak out on Monday night. Gifts for Noah and Lisa wouldn't be a problem, but he had no idea what he'd buy for Jonathan.

A few minutes later, Jonathan's car was empty and the packages were all in the basement. Lisa asked Ed, "Do you mind if two more join us tonight?"

"Two more what?" Ed asked. He'd planned to go out to dinner that night with Lisa and Noah because Jonathan was having dinner with his old college friend and fuck buddy. Ed was trying hard to keep his voice calm and normal, but when he thought about Jonathan and Joel, it felt like his head was ready to explode.

"*People*, you fool," she said, shaking her head. "Jonathan and Joel. I invited them to join us tonight."

Ed rubbed his chin. Lisa's voice sounded too casual and forced,

128

as if she were up to something she didn't want him to know.

"It's fine with me," Ed said, "as long as Jonathan doesn't mind. I thought he wanted to have some privacy with his good old buddy. Actually, I'd like to meet Joel. He sounds like a great guy." He was being facetious now, but in a subtle way that only Jonathan would recognize.

Jonathan gave him a look and said, "It's fine with *me*. I'm actually looking forward to it. I think you guys are going to be great buddies." Then he leaned forward and stared at Ed's face. "But you'd better shave first. You look a little scruffy."

Ed smiled. He knew Jonathan was teasing. He also knew how much Jonathan loved it when he rubbed his five o'clock shadow back and forth across his neck. "I think I'll stay like this," he said. "I like being casual and rough looking."

"Suit yourself," Jonathan said. "It's of no concern to me." Then he poked Noah in the arm and said, "C'mon, buddy, let's take Tucker out for a quick walk while your dad changes his clothes. Even though he's not going to shower and shave, I'm sure he's going to put on a decent pair of pants and a fresh shirt."

Ed was wearing the camouflage shorts and a paint-stained T-shirt he'd been wearing all day. He smiled and tugged his shorts. "I think I look okay. I don't think old Joel will mind."

Lisa rolled her eyes. "Just go up and change, Ed. You look like a slob."

Ed looked to Noah for support, but Noah pressed his lips together and nodded in agreement with Lisa. "You could use a shower, Dad."

* * * *

A half hour later, Ed jogged down the steps in a pair of fresh jeans, a white dress shirt and black dress shoes. He was carrying his best black sport jacket over his arm, and he'd styled his short, sandy blond hair with product. He'd shaved, showered, and splashed cologne on his face. Normally, he would have worn a polo shirt and a leather jacket, but he wasn't sure what to expect with this Joel guy. He pictured him as the Ivy League type, with thick blond hair, a double-breasted navy blazer with an emblem, and loafers with tassels.

Lisa, Noah, and Tucker were outside waiting in the car. Ed heard the powder room door open and Jonathan came down the hall. He put on the sport jacket and reached for his car keys on the table.

When Jonathan saw him, he stopped in the middle of the hall and said, "You look good. I like that jacket."

Ed shrugged his shoulders. "I figured you didn't want to be seen with a slob."

Jonathan leaned forward and whispered, "*I* never said you

looked like a slob. Lisa said that. You look great now, but I think you looked just as great before you changed and shaved. You know, you were wearing those old shorts the first time I met you."

"I was?"

Jonathan nodded. "I thought they were sexy then, and I think they are even sexier now."

When Jonathan said things like that, Ed's eyebrows usually went up. How did he remember these things? So Ed reached forward and grabbed the back of his head. He pulled Jonathan's face to his and kissed him on the mouth. They locked tongues and Ed placed his palm on the small of Jonathan's back. For a moment, Ed's strength increased and Jonathan's arms fell limp.

But then Jonathan pressed his palms on Ed's chest and said, "We have to go now." Then he grabbed Ed's crotch, squeezed it twice, and headed out the front door with a huge smile on his face. Jonathan was wearing low-rise jeans with a wide black leather belt. The pockets hugged his small, round ass. It was the hottest ass Ed had ever seen. He wanted to pull him back into the hall and sink his teeth into it. When he followed Jonathan out the door, he didn't even realize he was licking his lips.

They dropped Tucker off at the guest house and drove over to Joel's hotel. Lisa sat in the back seat with Noah and Jonathan was up front with Ed. When they pulled up to the lobby and Ed saw that Joel was staying at the hotel where Jonathan was staying, he raised his eyebrows and gave Jonathan a knowing look. Jonathan must have been reading his mind, because he turned in the opposite direction and sighed out loud.

Joel was waiting at the lobby door. Lisa opened the back window of the Range Rover and waved in his direction. When the lobby door opened and he jogged toward them, Ed grabbed the steering wheel with one hand and made a fist with the other. The guy was even better looking than Ed had imagined. His hair was light blond, his face was tanned and he had one of those naturally athletic bodies that jog with ease. Nothing jiggled or bounced; his hair hardly moved. His eyes were so blue you could see them from a distance. He was dressed casually in a black cotton shirt and tight beige jeans. The bulge between his legs was enormous. And when he reached the car and smiled, two perfect dimples formed on both of his cheeks. He reminded Ed of Australian actor Simon Baker.

Ed tried to force a smile, but his heart was thumping and his stomach was turning in circles. He couldn't stop picturing him in bed with Jonathan.

At first, it was awkward. Joel sat in the back seat with Lisa and Noah, and Jonathan introduced him on the way to the restaurant. Joel's voice was clear and deep, and his handshake was strong and solid. The fact that he had tons of money and a great job made him even seem like the most perfect man on earth. Ed wanted to fold himself in half and disappear under the front seat. He'd never felt so old and been so intimidated in his entire life.

Then Ed noticed a sudden change in Lisa's mannerisms. It started in the car, and became more obvious when they were inside the restaurant. She sat across the table from Joel. She spoke softly to him, and batted her eyelashes. When Joel spoke, she sat back, looked into his eyes, and listened to his words as if no one else was in the room. He made a few bad jokes, and she laughed so hard she almost choked on her drink. Ed looked at Jonathan, and Jonathan shrugged his shoulders with a mouthful of food. When Ed looked at Noah, Noah was rolling his eyes and making a face at Lisa.

Joel was just as bad. He didn't talk about his college days with Jonathan once. He barely said a word to Jonathan during the entire dinner. He kept smiling and staring at Lisa the whole time, paying her compliments and asking questions about her life in New York. When it came out that Lisa loved to go to the Met, he slapped his knee and said, "Isn't that something," three times in a row. When she mentioned that her favorite novel of all time was *On the Road*, and he said that was *his* all-time favorite novel, too, Ed almost gagged on his pork chop. Evidently, Lisa had forgotten to mention the real reason she'd wanted Joel and Jonathan to go to dinner with them: so she could get into Joel's pants that night.

By the time the waiter brought the check, Ed was smiling so wide his gums were showing. Joel was definitely straight and he was only interested in Lisa. He'd barely said two words to Jonathan all night. Ed paid the entire bill and left a huge tip for the waiter. He was so happy that he actually patted Joel on the back on the way out of the restaurant and said, "I'm so glad I had a chance to meet you. You're a great guy, Joel. I wish you could stay and spend Christmas with us."

On the way to the car, Lisa pulled Ed aside and said, "Joel and I are going to walk around town for a while, and then we'll take a taxi back to his hotel. Would you mind staying at the guest house with Noah tonight?"

Ed smiled and hugged her. "Mind? He's my son. Of course I'll stay with him. You just go and have all the fun you want. You deserve it. I have an even better idea for Noah." Then he jogged over to the car where the others were waiting and said, "Noah, Lisa and Joel are going to walk around town. How would you like to come back home with me and camp out for the night? We'll get Tucker on the way."

Noah smiled and jumped up and down. "Can Jonathan come, too?" he asked. "We can all camp out in the living room."

"Ah well," Ed said. "It's up to Jonathan if he wants to come back with us. He might not want to sleep on the living room floor."

Jonathan stood there staring at Ed. Noah tugged on his sleeve and said, "Please, Jonathan? We'll have fun. C'mon."

Ed smirked at Jonathan and tilted his head to the side.

Jonathan looked down at Noah and said, "I'm not sure, buddy. Can I light a fire and plug in the Christmas tree?"

Noah looked at Ed for permission, and Ed nodded yes.

"Then let's go get Tucker," Jonathan said. "I have a feeling he's going to love this."

Chapter Eleven

The day before Christmas Eve, Jonathan woke up an hour early and drove to Ed's house before the film crew and the construction workers arrived. It was a cool and rainy Tuesday morning. There was a light mist in the air and the sun hadn't fully risen yet.

Jonathan and Ed hadn't been together since Friday, and that had only been a quick blow job for Ed when the workers left for lunch. On Saturday they spent the night camping out with Noah and Tucker on the living room floor, on Sunday they took Noah to the zoo because Lisa was still with Joel at the hotel, and on Monday construction ran into overtime and didn't end until ten o'clock at night. There had been a problem with the installation of a bathtub in the second-floor guest bathroom. The antique ball and clawfoot tub didn't fit and Ed had another tantrum. They had to rebuild the wall behind the tub, because Ed had insisted on that particular tub. It was great for the TV show, though: you couldn't predict what would happen next with old houses.

So Jonathan decided to surprise Ed in bed that morning before everyone arrived for work. He knew it might be the last time they could be together for a while. Noah's Christmas show was that night, and the next day Noah was off from school until after New

Year's.

He pulled into the driveway and switched off the engine. He got out of the car slowly, closing the door with a small click. He crossed to the garage door and found the hidden house key. It was under a large rock beside a round boxwood bush, where Ed had showed him one afternoon when he'd picked Noah up from school. Then he slipped in through the back door and crept up the back staircase. He was planning to knock on the bedroom door first. He didn't want Ed to think someone had broken into the house.

The house was dark and quiet. When he reached the master bedroom, he removed all his clothes and left them in a heap beside the door. He stepped into the room on the tips of his toes and saw the bed was empty. He turned and noticed the bathroom door was shut. There was a sound of running water. Ed was taking a shower; he probably hadn't slept all night. Jonathan decided not to surprise him in the bathroom and scare him to death, so he crossed to a desk in the corner of the room and found a notepad and a pen. In bold print he wrote, "Come back to bed!!" Then he slipped the note under the bathroom door and climbed into Ed's bed.

The bed was still warm; the pillows smelled like Ed's spicy deodorant and woodsy hair product. He buried his face in Ed's pillow and took a deep breath. He'd never met a man with such a distinct smell. It was the cologne and deodorant mixed with his own body oils, creating an individual aroma all its own. It reminded Jonathan of allspice and cedar and burning leaves in the fall.

A minute later, the water stopped running and he heard the shower door slam shut. There was a moment of silence, and then the bathroom door opened and Ed stepped into the bedroom. He had a black bath towel around his neck and his body was dripping with water. He was holding the note in his left hand and scratching his penis with the right. "Oh, Jonathan, it's you," he said.

Jonathan pulled the covers back, exposing half of his naked body, and said, "Were you expecting someone else?"

"Yeah, Bill the plumber," he said. He walked toward the bed and smiled. Bill the plumber was about three hundred pounds and wore his jeans below his waist. Whenever he bent over to pick up a tool, everyone nearby saw the crack of his ass.

"Sorry," Jonathan said, spreading his legs wider. "It's just me."

Ed pulled the towel off his neck and started to rub his wet head. "I'm glad I didn't jerk off in the shower this morning," he said.

"Don't do that," Jonathan said. "Don't dry your hair or any-thing else. You look good all wet." Jonathan was one of those guys who trimmed their pubic hairs and shaved their bodies regularly. But Ed wasn't. The sandy blond patch of hair above his penis was soaked with water and matted down, and the hair on his legs stuck to his skin. He wasn't a hairy man at all, but the hair he had was in all the right places.

Ed dropped the towel and climbed up on the bed. He pulled the covers off Jonathan and lifted his right leg over his naked body. He remained on his knees. He was smiling and his penis was almost completely erect. When he rested his weight on his hands and bent forward to kiss him, a drop of water fell on Jonathan's cheek. Ed licked it off, then shoved his tongue into Jonathan's mouth.

While they kissed, Jonathan grabbed Ed's penis with one hand and held the back of his wet head with the other. His thick hair was slippery and cold, but his wide penis was warm and hot. Jonathan jerked it up and down with slow, careful pulls. The tighter he held it in his palm, the deeper Ed's tongue went into his mouth.

Then Ed pressed his wet body against Jonathan. He went down hard and wrapped his strong arms around him. Jonathan wrapped his arms around Ed's neck and spread his legs as wide as they would go. Ed felt different that morning: stronger and sharper. His movements were calculated and connected. When they rolled back and forth on the mattress and kissed, he pressed his palm against the small of Jonathan's back with such force, Jonathan felt completely overpowered. When he grabbed Jonathan's ass hard and spread it apart, the hairs on the back of his neck stood up. Jonathan felt both helpless and protected in his strapping arms. The rougher Ed handled him, the more he wanted to submit.

Ed had always been aggressive with him. But this time it was different. This time it felt as if Ed was purposely taking control — without asking for permission. And Jonathan didn't want him to stop. He could have remained on his back all day, kissing Ed's lips and squeezing the muscles in his arms.

When Ed finally did stop kissing him, he said, "Get up on your knees and spread your legs." Jonathan grabbed his hand and followed his directions. Ed's voice even sounded different. It had a deep, dark tone Jonathan hadn't heard before.

When Jonathan arched his back, Ed grabbed both sides of his ass and buried his face in the trenches. It happened so unexpectedly fast, Jonathan moaned out loud. His eyes opened wide and his head went back. Ed started to lick and chew the lips of his opening. Jonathan swallowed and gasped for air. He clutched the sheets to keep his balance.

But it was futile for him to fight such a strong force. Ed's face pushed into his ass so hard that Jonathan wound up flat on his stomach, facing the foot of the bed. Ed only lifted his head to take deep breaths. He continued to chew and lick; he squeezed and massaged Jonathan's ass cheeks until he thought they turned red. Then, just when Jonathan thought it couldn't get any better, Ed stuck his tongue into Jonathan's body and rolled it in circles.

When he finally stopped, Jonathan's ass was numb with pleasure and his body vibrated with pre-orgasmic sensations. "Are you ready for more?" Ed asked.

"Uh-huh," Jonathan said, nodding his head up and down at the foot of the bed.

Ed stretched across the bed and pulled a tube of lubricant from the nightstand. He lathered his erection fast, then coated Jonathan's opening. He shoved two fingers into his hole and poked them around a few times to make sure it was slick. Jonathan closed his eyes and moaned again. Then Ed pulled his fingers out and shoved his penis inside Jonathan's body with one hard, deep thrust.

"Ah," Ed sighed, "this is my favorite position. Is it okay like this?"

Jonathan nodded yes. He could barely open his mouth to speak. "Yes. Don't stop," he said. This was Jonathan's favorite position, too. He didn't have to do anything but lie there and concentrate on tightening his sphincter muscle while Ed nailed him to the mattress.

Ed assumed a position that looked as if he were going to do pushups on Jonathan's back, then started bucking his hips and sliding his penis in and out of Jonathan's body. Ed supported the weight of his upper body with his arms and locked his elbows tight. His large hands made deep indentations in the mattress and the sheets gathered at his fingertips. The only part of Ed's body that moved was his pelvis. It rocked and hammered with a constant rhythm that increased with speed and intensity.

Fifteen minutes later, while the mattress bounced and Jonathan's head jerked up and down, Ed groaned and said, "I'm close, man."

Jonathan spread his legs wider. He bent his legs at the knee and his calves went up. His own penis was rubbing against the sheets and Ed's penis was hitting his most sensitive spot, a deep place inside his body that rocked his world. His orgasm had been building from the minute Ed had entered him. "Me too," he shouted. "Harder, Ed." Then he curled his toes and bit the sheets.

They climaxed together, and Jonathan never touched his own erection once. When Ed's penis erupted, something deep in Jonathan's body jumped and he came all over the sheets beneath him. It wasn't something that happened to Jonathan often.

Ed remained inside. He fell on Jonathan's back and kissed the nape of his neck. "Damn," he said, "that was intense."

Jonathan sighed and stretched his arms over the end of the bed. His body was still filled with Ed's penis and his own strong post-orgasmic sensations. "I'm glad I came over here this morning," he said.

Ed was rocking his hips in slow circles now. "I'm glad you did, too. I've been dying to sink my teeth into that ass."

"Then why didn't you do it sooner?" Jonathan asked. He turned to look back at Ed.

Ed shrugged. "I can get kind of rough sometimes. I didn't want to scare you away, I guess."

Jonathan clamped down on Ed's semi-erect penis so it wouldn't slide out. He gripped it so hard Ed's head jerked to the left. Ed's voice sounded innocent now, almost apologetic. So Jonathan smiled and said, "You're an excellent lover, Ed. The best I've ever known."

Ed tilted his head and made a face. "Really?"

But Jonathan didn't have a chance to answer. There was a loud knock on the front door and Ed turned to see what time it was. It was after eight and the workers were coming in to lay marble in one of the second-floor bathrooms.

Jonathan released his grip and Ed slid out of his body. Ed jumped off his back and said, "I'll go wash up and get dressed fast, then I'll go down and stall them until you come down."

Jonathan smiled and stretched his legs. "Okay," he said.

Ed stood up and said, "And stop looking that way."

"What way?"

"As if you just got fucked," Ed said. "It's all over your face. You always have a ridiculous expression after you've been fucked."

Jonathan forced a frown and said, "How's this?"

Ed put his hands on his hips and shook his head. "Not very convincing. You still look like you just got nailed."

He looked at Ed and stared between his legs. "Well, this is the best I can do."

* * * *

That night Noah sang his solo in the Christmas show. A classmate of his, Katie Lungwort, fawned over him on the way out to the parking lot. "You were just wonderful, Noah," she said. "You were better than everyone else." She had long blond hair, bright blue eyes, and a soft smile. She was wearing a pink costume for the show with long white ribbons on the sleeves.

Noah shrugged his shoulders and looked down at his shoes. "Thanks," he said, shoving his hands into the pockets of his navy blue suit pants.

Katie smiled and handed him a small piece of paper. "Here's my phone number. You can call me if you want."

Noah took the paper and shoved it into his pocket. He shrugged again and said, "Okay."

Then Katie wished him a merry Christmas and skipped off to find her family.

Ed looked at Lisa, and then he said to Noah, "I didn't know you and Katie were such good friends."

"Hey, neither did I," Lisa said.

Noah kicked his left foot and looked up to Jonathan for support. Jonathan put his hand on Noah's shoulder and said, "Katie's a nice girl. They are just good friends." Then he gave Ed a knowing look and changed the subject. "Let's go back to the house for some coffee or something. Tucker is all alone." He didn't want Jonathan and Lisa to make a big thing about Katie and embarrass Noah. Noah had been confiding in him about Katie while they'd been rehearsing his solo for the show. Noah had his first real crush on a girl, and he was very sensitive about it.

Ed poked Lisa in the arm and said, "Ah well, yes, Tucker is waiting for us." Then he put his arm around his son and said, "You were really good tonight, buddy. I know how hard you and Jonathan worked on that song. It was worth it."

On the way to the car, Lisa leaned into Jonathan's side and said, "Did you see Ed's expression when that little girl gave Noah her phone number? I thought he was going to fall over on the sidewalk." She talked through the side of her mouth and giggled. "I'm not sure he's ready for this yet. Noah's growing up."

When they reached the house a few minutes later, Noah pointed to the front window and said, "See, Dad, how good the tree looks in the window from the street? You can see all the lights and it looks just like Christmas." Noah had asked if they could plug in the tree before they'd left for the show. Ed said he didn't like leaving the lights on while they were out, but he'd agreed to do it just that once.

Ed switched off the engine and opened his door. "You were right, buddy," he said. "It's much better there than next to the fireplace."

Noah continued to stare at the window. "I think Dad would have liked our tree this year," he said.

He was talking about Jake again. Jonathan's heart sank to his stomach. He looked at Lisa, frowned, and pressed his palm to his throat. Lisa lowered her head to her lap and smiled. They never knew when Noah was going to say something innocent that wound up leaving everyone speechless.

But this time Ed didn't change the subject and avoid Noah. He smiled at Noah and looked into his eyes. "I think he would have liked our tree this year, too, son."

Tucker was waiting for them at the front door. They could hear his paws clicking on the tile floor in the hallway. Ed unlocked the door and went in first to flip on the hall lights. Tucker's tail was wagging and he was panting. When he saw Noah, he jumped past Ed and ran down the front walk to lick his face. Tucker was so happy to see him he lunged forward and knocked him down on the grass. He licked his entire face twice.

Jonathan and Lisa stood there laughing. But Ed lowered his voice and said, "Grab his collar, buddy. I don't want him outside without a leash."

Jonathan and Lisa turned to go inside. Noah laughed and reached for Tucker's collar. But just before he could loop his fingers beneath the black leather, a siren sounded. It came from nowhere and two police cars rushed past the house. Their red lights were rolling in circles and their sirens blaring.

When Jonathan turned back to see what was happening, he saw Noah running down the front lawn. One arm was stretched out and he was shouting, "Tucker, come back here."

But he stopped short at the end of the lawn, because Tucker was already down the street and out of sight. He turned back and spread his arms wide. He stared at Jonathan. His small face turned red and tears fell from his eyes. "He's gone, Jonathan! He's gone." Then he fell to his knees and started sobbing.

Chapter Twelve

Before Ed went out looking for Tucker in his car, he wanted to take Lisa and Noah back to the guest cottage. Noah was sitting on the front steps next to Jonathan with his elbows on his knees and his head in his hands. But he refused to leave the house. "What if Tucker comes back here and there's no one home, Dad?" he said. He pointed his small finger down toward the sidewalk and moved it up and down. "He'd never go back to that guest house. *This* is where he lives. *This* is his home."

Jonathan looked at Ed and said, "He has a point. It might be a good idea for Noah to sleep here tonight." It was the day before Christmas Eve, and the boy's dog had just run off after a police car. To send him back to a rented guest house for a good night's sleep would have been futile. But he knew Ed meant well, and that Ed was only thinking of Noah's best interests. Jonathan knew it wasn't his place to get involved, but he had to say something on Noah's behalf. The poor kid was devastated.

And thankfully, Lisa agreed. "You and Jonathan can go look for him," she said, "We'll go upstairs to your room, Ed, and wait." The house wasn't ready to live in yet. The upstairs bathrooms still weren't finished and the only bed in the house was in Ed's room.

Ed sighed and squatted down to look Noah in the eye. He grabbed his hands and said, "We'll get him, buddy. Stop worrying. You can spend the night here in your own home." Then he looked up at Jonathan and said, "I have a couple of flashlights in the garage. I'll get them. You go wait in the car."

Jonathan looked at him and tilted his head. "I'm going on foot," he said. "It will be easier to spot him that way. We'll keep in touch with our cell phones and meet up later. If you find him first, call me. I'll do the same."

Noah lifted his head and tugged on Ed's pants. "Can I go with Jonathan, Dad?" he asked. "If Tucker sees me, he'll come back right away."

Ed frowned. "No, Noah. You stay here with Lisa. It's too late and you've had enough for one day."

"Your Dad's right, buddy," Jonathan said. "I can cover a lot of ground alone. I'm fast and I'm used to walking all the time in New York. Tucker knows me, and he'll come to me if he sees me."

Noah lowered his head to his shoes and nodded yes. Lisa sat down next to him and put her arms around him. "Call us if you find him," Noah said.

Ed and Jonathan said at the same time, "Of course we will."

Then Ed went into the house to get Tucker's retractable leash from the hall closet. He also found an old leash they'd used when he was a puppy. When he came out, he handed the retractable leash to Jonathan and said, "I'll call you in about a half hour to find out where you are."

He called Jonathan every half hour for an update. Each time the phone rang, Jonathan pulled it from his back pocket and looked up at the sky, hoping for good news. Then he'd hang up a minute later, frown, and continue searching. Jonathan walked for miles. He peeked over fences, snooped through shrubbery, and walked up and down dark driveways. If he heard a dog bark at a house he passed by, he knocked on the front door and asked if they'd seen Tucker. He called the dog's name, slapped his thigh, and whistled. At one point, about six blocks away from Ed's house, he saw a police car cruising down the street and he flagged the cop down. He gave him a description of Tucker and Ed's address. The cop said he'd keep his eyes open, but couldn't promise anything. Jonathan thanked him and continued walking.

By two o'clock in the morning, Ed called and asked where he was. When Jonathan told him he was nearly seven miles away, Ed wanted to pick him up there and go home for the night. He was about five miles away in the other direction. But Jonathan refused; he couldn't imagine going back to the house and telling Noah he hadn't been able to find Tucker. So he told Ed he'd start walking home and that he'd backtrack along the way in case he'd missed something. Maybe he'd find him sitting on someone's front steps, lost and wondering how to get home.

At one point, only two blocks away from Ed's, he saw the shadow of a large dog on someone's front lawn. His heart raced and he jogged in the dog's direction. It had to be Tucker. When he called out his name, the dog stopped and stared at him for a moment. He tilted his head sideways and whimpered.

Then a woman's voice called, "Spody, c'mon inside now." The dog turned and ran to the front door. And when he was under the porch light, Jonathan saw he was an Irish setter, not a black lab.

When he reached Ed's house, he was still alone. He placed the retractable leash on the hall table and sighed. It was almost five o'clock in the morning. His feet ached and his voice was sore from calling Tucker's name. Ed was in the dining room waiting for him. He was sitting in the dark at the head of the table with his arms folded across his chest.

Jonathan sat down at the other end of the table and stared down at his feet. The backs of his legs were actually tingling with aches and pains and he couldn't wait to remove his shoes. He asked Ed, "Where's Noah?" He'd had this image of Noah sitting on the front steps the entire time he'd been out looking.

"He's upstairs sleeping," Ed said. "Lisa's with him."

Then Ed stood up and yawned. "C'mon," he said. "Let's try to get some sleep. I'll grab a few covers and pillows that are in boxes in the garage."

They slept on the living room floor in front of the fireplace. But they only slept for about two hours, because Noah came running down the stairs looking for Tucker at seven o'clock. He was still wearing the same clothes he'd worn to the school Christmas show. His sandy blond hair was tangled and his eyes were still red and puffy from crying. Ed and Jonathan were sleeping about six feet apart. Ed was on his stomach and Jonathan was on his back. They were also still wearing the same clothes they'd worn the night before.

When Jonathan heard him coming down the stairs, he poked Ed in the arm and said, "You'd better wake up."

Ed grunted and turned to his side. Noah was standing at his feet. He looked at his father and said, "You didn't find him, did you?"

Ed shook his head and sat up straight. "We'll start looking again this morning as soon as I have some coffee and we get you back to the guest house to wash up and change your clothes."

Then Jonathan sat up and rubbed his eyes. "You can come with us this time, too, Noah," he said. "Maybe if he hears your voice he'll come faster."

Noah shrugged his shoulders and said, "Okay." He wasn't

crying anymore. But when he turned to leave the room, he looked back and Ed and said, "This is almost as bad as when Dad died."

* * * *

While Lisa went shopping for food for their Christmas dinner—Jonathan thought ahead and gave her a detailed list so she wouldn't get confused—Ed, Jonathan, and Noah searched for Tucker all day. It was the day before Christmas and the streets and roads were jammed with people shopping and running last-minute errands. They drove through back alleys and down streets they never knew existed. They parked and walked on foot, asking people on the street if they'd seen Tucker. Noah was carrying a small photo of him in his little-boy wallet, the one with superheroes on the outside flap. They checked animal shelters and veterinarian offices in case someone else had found Tucker and dropped him off.

But it was all for nothing. It was as if Tucker had dropped off the planet in the flash of an eye.

On Christmas Eve, they went out to dinner. Ed had made reservations three weeks earlier at one of San Francisco's best restaurants on the wharf, but no one felt like eating. Noah sat there, kicking his feet and staring at his plate, expressionless. Lisa kept looking at Ed and sighing out loud.

Jonathan finally said, "You know, Noah, when I was about your age I had a dog named Homer. We called him 'Old Homer,' because he looked like an old dog from the time he was a puppy. He was a rough old schnauzer who was allergic to fleas and couldn't stand more than five minutes in the car. He was fine for the first five minutes, but when the car started moving faster, he'd jump down on the floor and start shaking. He hated the car."

Noah stared at Jonathan and asked, "What happened to him?" He'd been playing with his string beans, shoving them into his mashed potatoes as if he were building a barricade on his plate.

Jonathan smiled. "One afternoon we left the gate open by accident, and Old Homer disappeared. No one could even remember who did it. It just happened."

"Just like Tucker," Noah said.

"That's right," Jonathan said. "He just took off on his own. We looked everywhere, all over town. And we didn't find him. I was devastated. I couldn't eat or sleep. And then one day, about three weeks later, a woman on the other side of town called my mother saying she'd found him. Old Homer had a name tag with an address and phone number, just like Tucker's, and he'd turned up on her doorstep one morning."

Noah sat on the edge of his seat, still staring at Jonathan. "Did you get him back?"

Jonathan nodded. "Yes, we did. He was thin and he had a few bruises, but we got him back and he lived to be the ripe old age of nineteen years old. We never knew what happened to him while he was gone. We figured he'd just run off and gotten lost on the railroad tracks. The woman who found him lived near the tracks."

Lisa stopped eating and said, "That's amazing."

Jonathan smiled and said, "I'm telling you this because I don't want you to give up hope, buddy. I never thought I'd see Old Homer again. But I did."

Ed said, "Tucker also has an identification chip in his ear. So if anyone finds him, anywhere in the city, we can always locate him that way, too."

Noah thought for a moment, then asked his father, "Can we post his picture around town, Dad? Maybe he'll turn up just like Old Homer."

"We'll post his picture, I'll take out ads in the newspaper, and I'll contact all the vets I know in the city to keep an eye open for him," Ed said.

"I'll post it to Craigslist," Lisa said.

Noah smiled for the first time since Tucker had run off. "Well, if Jonathan can find *Old Homer*, I think we can get Tucker back, too." Then he reached for his fork and started to eat his chicken.

Lisa smiled at Jonathan, and Ed looked him in the eye and said, "Thanks for telling that story. It even makes me feel better."

Jonathan shrugged and said, "I really did think Old Homer was gone, but I got him back anyway."

After dinner, Ed dropped Lisa and Noah off at the guest house and said good night. Jonathan waited in the car and he walked them to the door to make sure Noah was okay. When Ed came back, he started the car and looked at Jonathan. He reached down, grabbed his thigh, and said, "It's late and we're both exhausted. Why don't you just spend the night? I don't want you going back to the hotel at all. If you need a change of clothes, you can borrow something of mine in the morning."

Jonathan smiled and said, "Aren't you worried about what people might think?"

Ed threw his hands in the air and said, "I'm so tired right now I don't give a fuck what anyone thinks anymore. Just come home and spend the night with me. I always sleep when you're there, and tonight I want to sleep. I don't want to lie there staring at the ceiling all night."

Jonathan reached between his legs and grabbed his crotch. Whenever Ed hiked up his pants and sat down, he was one of those men who showed a huge bulge between his legs. Jonathan squeezed it a few times. It felt firm and doughy. "Is that all you want to do?"

Ed laughed and adjusted himself in the seat so Jonathan could get a better grip on his package. He said, "Maybe." Then he slipped the car into gear and backed out of the driveway with Jonathan's hand between his legs.

A few minutes later, they reached Ed's house and Jonathan was still holding his crotch. He'd squeezed it and massaged it all the way back to the house. Now he was holding more than just a soft, thick package. Ed's penis had grown to a full erection and it pulsed up and down in Jonathan's palm. Jonathan pulled down his zipper and pulled it out of his pants. He wrapped his hand around the shaft and held it tight. Ed spread his legs wider and rested his head on the back of the seat. "You want to do it here in the car?"

"No," Jonathan said. "I want to hold on to it all the way into the house and up to the bedroom."

"You're going to have to let go when I get out of the car," Ed said.

Jonathan smiled. "No," he said. "You're going to climb over the seat and get out through my door so I don't have to let go."

"I'm older than you are," Ed said. "What if I can't get my leg over the center console?"

"You're not *that* old," Jonathan said. Then he unbuckled his seat belt and leaned over. He tightened his grip around Ed's erection and lowered his head, then slipped half of Ed's penis into his mouth and sucked on it a couple of times. When his head went up again, he smiled and licked his lips. He tugged on Ed's erection and said, "Now lift those legs over the console and follow me up-stairs to the bedroom so I can get down on my knees and work that big thing the right way."

Ed almost lost his balance and fell back, but he made it over the center console and out of the car. When they were standing in the driveway, he kissed Jonathan on the mouth and they slowly walked toward the back door. Jonathan held his shaft and walked backwards. Ed kissed him and held the back of his head to guide him up the back steps. When they were inside the house, Jonathan turned around, repositioned his grip, and yanked him upstairs.

When they were in the bedroom, Jonathan went down on his knees and unfastened Ed's pants. He pulled down his zipper and they fell to his ankles. He ran the side of his face up and down his hairy thigh for a moment, taking deep breaths to absorb his tweedy, masculine aroma. Ed was wearing white boxer shorts; they were all bunched up and his erection was sticking out of the opening. There were few sights more wonderful than seeing a huge dick pop from a pair of white boxer shorts. Jonathan stuck out his tongue and licked the head, then said, "See? Walking around with me holding your dick wasn't so hard, and you're not too old to do anything. Besides, I like pulling you around by the dick. I should do that more often."

Ed's eyebrows went up and he smiled. "You really do like my

dick, don't you?"

Jonathan nodded and licked the head. "I can't get enough of it."

Ed spread his legs wider and ran his fingers through Jonathan's thick, dark hair. He lowered his voice and said, "Get naked."

Jonathan released his grip and stripped for him on the floor. He was wearing a black dress shirt; he opened the top three buttons and pulled it over his head. His cream-colored slacks came off fast; he pulled his shoes and socks off with them. When he slipped off his white briefs, he did it slowly. Then he tossed them up to Ed and smiled.

Ed reached for them in mid-air. He clutched the underwear Jonathan had been wearing all evening and he smiled so widely, his dimples turned into creases. Then he pressed the white cotton briefs to his nose and inhaled so hard his chest rounded forward.

Jonathan lifted his head and watched him. He pressed both palms on Ed's thighs and ran them up and down with slow, even strokes. He'd never had a lover who had done something like this in front of him. He'd once caught a guy sniffing his underwear when he thought Jonathan wasn't watching. Jonathan had done the same thing on the sly many times; most normal gay men would. But no one had ever inhaled the scent of his underwear while he'd watched.

When Ed removed the briefs from his face and tossed them on

the floor, he said, "Take off my shoes and socks now, then take off my pants."

Jonathan, still on his knees, leaned forward and untied his black shoes. He loosened the laces, held Ed's ankle with one hand and reached for the heel of the shoe with the other. He pulled it off slowly, then removed his black sock. Ed's foot was soft and warm and smelled like shoe leather. He had large toes, a deep arch, and a wide instep. Jonathan didn't have a foot fetish, but he thought Ed's were the sexiest he'd ever seen.

After he removed the other shoe, Ed removed his shirt. It landed behind him on the bed. When Ed was naked, Jonathan rose up on his knees and took Ed's penis with the tips of his fingers. His thumb slowly massaged the thick vein on the bottom with light strokes. Without moving his head, he lifted his eyes to Ed's face and took the thick erection into his mouth. And when the head hit the back of his throat and Ed's pubic hairs were pressed to his lips, he opened his mouth a little wider and sucked up his ball sack, too.

He guzzled and sucked on Ed's entire package this way for a few minutes. From the moaning coming from Ed, he had to wonder if anyone had ever sucked his penis and his balls at the same time. Ed just stood there groaning, taking swallow breaths. He held Jonathan's head in his hands and pressed hard on his ears.

When Jonathan finally removed Ed's balls from his mouth, he

only did it because the sides of his face were hurting. But he didn't remove Ed's penis from his mouth. He began the serious cocksucking. If he'd said that out loud, *serious cocksucking*, it would have sounded silly to anyone who didn't know or understand anything about gay culture or gay sex. But Jonathan, like any gay man, had always believed there was a difference between good cocksucking and a dreadful, forced blow job. The bad ones, given by those who really didn't like doing it, amounted to nothing more than following the expected motions. But Jonathan loved it: he liked the feel of it, the taste of it, and the smell of it. And he loved Ed's penis more than any other penis in the world. So he pressed both palms on the bottom of Ed's flat stomach and moved his head back and forth. His cheeks indented and his tongue gripped the bottom. He wanted to please him and show him how much he loved his body. Saliva dripped from the left corner of his mouth; loud, sloppy suction noises came from his lips.

He sucked this way until he could taste pre-come on his tongue. It wasn't as salty as it was with other men. Ed's had a sweet under taste that made it special. Ed grabbed the top of his head and said, "Let's fuck."

While Jonathan got up on the bed, Ed lathered his erection with lube. Then he got into bed and said, "Lie down on your right side and lift your left leg up high."

Jonathan smiled and followed Ed's orders. When he was on his side, his lifted his left leg up high and pointed his toes. Ed grabbed his ankle and lifted it even higher, then he crawled between Jonathan's legs and shoved his erection into his ass crack. Jonathan was used to Ed's penis by then: the head slipped into his hole and the shaft went up his ass with one easy push. When it was in deep, he rested his ankle on Ed's shoulder and said, "Come inside me, Ed...breed me." He didn't scream this sentence. He said it softly, almost as a stage whisper.

He wanted Ed to pound and hammer and slam his ass until he filled his body. For Jonathan, this was the ultimate erotic pleasure. He even liked all the tacky clichés: man-juice, nectar, cream, et cetera. He'd been with guys who had fucked well with condoms, but always had to pull out at the end and jerk off without the condom in order to climax. And for Jonathan, getting fucked this way was all right, but never as wonderful as when the guy actually fucked long enough to come inside his body. Condoms ruined the fullness of the experience. You had to use them, but that didn't make them feel good. Jonathan had always practiced safe sex with strangers; he'd never lived in a time when safe sex wasn't an option. But now he knew Ed was safe and disease free, and he knew how much Ed liked to fuck and come inside him. So all he wanted to do was spread his legs, lie there, and take a load from the man with whom he was falling in love.

Ed remained in an upright position, on his knees, resting on his haunches with Jonathan's ankle on his shoulder. The only part of Ed's body that moved was his pelvis. He bucked it fast, pulling his erection in and out of Jonathan's hole. He leaned back as if he were handling a bronco. His rhythm remained stable and his erection rubbed the same parts of Jonathan's body over and over. The lips of Jonathan's opening vibrated toward climax and the insides of his canal came closer with each pound.

When Ed reached the end, he said, "I'm going off, man. I'm ready."

Jonathan clamped down on his penis. He held his own penis and started jerking it. "Come inside me, Ed," he said. "Come inside me." Just saying Ed's name brought him to the edge. Begging for this from the most breathtaking man he'd ever known made his eyes fall to the back of his head.

Ed grunted and made a face. He bucked fast about five times and emptied his load into Jonathan's body. This time it must have been a powerful orgasm. After he came, he continued to bang into Jonathan's body, with his mouth wide open and some loud groans. Jonathan's leg was bent so far back his knee almost touched his chin.

While Ed climaxed, Jonathan jerked off on the bed, repeating

Ed's name in a soft, simple whisper.

A drop of Ed's sweat fell on his stomach. Ed's took a deep breath and said, "I like this position. You're tight ass feels ten times tighter this way."

Jonathan threw his arms over his head and stretched. He could still feel Ed's full erection inside his body. He tightened the lips of his hole around Ed's shaft and said, "I like it, too."

Chapter Thirteen

After they took a shower together, they fell asleep in each
other's arms. Ed slept on his back and Jonathan rested his head on
Ed's chest. He pulled Jonathan as close to his body as he could,
and Jonathan lifted his right leg and wrapped it around Ed's waist.
The moment Ed closed his eyes, he drifted into a deep sleep and
didn't wake up until he saw daylight coming through the window.
He had an erection, and Jonathan was holding it in his soft, warm
hand.

"Did I snore last night?" Ed asked.

Jonathan snuggled closer and squeezed his penis. "I don't think
so, but I was so tired I'm not even sure." Then he ran his thumb
lightly over the head of Ed's penis and asked, "Did you sleep
okay?"

Ed smiled. "I haven't slept that well in a while. I feel great."
He spread his legs apart so Jonathan would continue to play with
it. Ed liked the way he was rubbing the head with his thumb. He
didn't want him to stop.

But Jonathan had other plans that morning. He let go of Ed's
dick and turned to his right. Then he reached beneath the bed and
pulled up a perfectly wrapped Christmas gift. The paper was gold

and the large bow was bright red. He handed it to Ed and said, "Merry Christmas. I got you something else for later when everyone exchanges gifts, but I wanted to give this to you now."

Ed tilted his head and said, "I got you something, too. But I don't have anything right now." He felt awkward. If he'd known they were going to be exchanging gifts in bed, he would have bought something else.

"I don't expect anything right now," Jonathan said. "This is just a sort of sexy, funny gift. It didn't cost much, but I think you're going to like it."

"Sexy?"

Jonathan nodded and said, "Open it."

Ed sat up higher against the pillows and removed the red bow first. He handed it to Jonathan and said, "Here, wrap this around your neck."

While Jonathan fastened the bow to his neck, Ed tore off the gold wrapping paper. It was a rectangular box with a lot of writing and clear cellophane on the top. He didn't bother to read what the box said. He looked down and pressed his lips together. He tilted his head and pressed his finger to his chin. It looked like a heavy duty flashlight. He smiled and said, "Ah well, I can always use another flashlight for the car." Then he kissed him on the lips and said, "Thank you."

"It's not a flashlight," Jonathan said. "It's a *fleshlight*."

"A *what*?"

Jonathan reached down for his penis again. It was semi-erect. He wrapped his fingers around it and said, "It's for your dick, not for your car."

"For my dick?"

Jonathan laughed. "I can't believe you've never heard of a fleshlight. Don't you watch porn? It's a sex toy." Then he took the box from Ed and pulled out what looked like a large flashlight with two small openings at both ends. There was a set of fake lips on one end, and a replica of a tight anus on the other.

Ed smiled. He'd never heard of a fleshlight. And he'd never been a huge fan of porn. Watching porn usually made him sigh and lower his eyes. He didn't want to watch DVDs of other guys having sex. He wanted the real thing. "How does it work?"

"I'll show you," Jonathan said. He reached for the lube on the nightstand and covered Ed's penis. When it was slick and shiny, he rubbed some lube on the anus opening of the fleshlight and said. "Lie back and close your eyes. You're going to like this."

Ed placed his hands behind his head and rested on the pillow. When his eyes were closed, Jonathan inserted Ed's penis into the opening of the fleshlight. The hole was soft and tight. His right leg jerked a few times and he took a deep breath. Jonathan moved it up and down slowly for the first few minutes, then went faster. It felt like a cross between a hand job and a blow job. The soft interior made Ed's balls tighten. Jonathan kept an even rhythm and his right arm never tired. The pleasure it created kept Ed on the edge of climax for such a long time he had to concentrate hard so he wouldn't come.

He finally opened his eyes and said, "I'm close, Jonathan. Get up now and sit on it." Then he slapped Jonathan on the ass twice so hard the smacks echoed in the almost-empty room.

Jonathan pulled the fleshlight off Ed's penis and straddled his body. He had a red mark on his ass where Ed had just slapped him. He looked so hot with the red Christmas bow around his neck that Ed reached forward and pinched both his nipples hard. Jonathan didn't complain. His head went back, his mouth opened, and he moaned with quick, awkward breaths.

But Jonathan didn't waste time moaning. He seemed to know Ed was close and he wanted to finish him off. So he straddled his legs and sat down in his erection. When it was all the way in and Ed could feel Jonathan's smooth ass on his balls, he placed one hand on Ed's chest and started to ride. He held his own penis with the other and squeezed his anal lips hard.

It didn't take long. Ed was sensitive and he'd been edging for a while. The red bow around his hot young lover's neck made his heart race. He clutched the sheets with his fists and sat up. Then he shouted, "Ah, ah, I'm coming."

Jonathan spread his legs wider and rode faster. And when Ed shot his load into Jonathan's body, Jonathan sprayed his all over Ed. It was as if Jonathan had no control over where his come landed, because most of it landed on Ed's face. Ed hadn't seen it coming; his eyes had been closed and he'd been concentrating on his own climax. It hit his right cheekbone with a light sting.

When Ed opened his eyes, Jonathan stared at his face and smiled. "Don't move," he said. "I'm sorry I hit you. I'll clean it up." His body went forward and he stuck out his tongue. He licked it all off Ed's face before it even had a chance to get cold.

* * * *

It was a good thing they'd showered and dressed fast that morning. Ed had tried to slip his finger into Jonathan's hole in the shower, but Jonathan had a feeling Noah would be there early that morning. "He's a kid, Ed," he'd said, "and it's Christmas morning. He'll be here soon, trust me. I don't want him to run upstairs and find us together like this. It wouldn't be right."

Ed pulled his finger out and sighed. "You're right. I don't know what I was thinking."

A few minutes later, while Ed was putting on his shoes, he heard a car pull into the driveway. It was Lisa and Noah. Jonathan was just finishing up changing the sheets and making the bed. He gave Ed a look and raised his eyebrow. Ed looked out the window and saw them lugging bags and packages from Lisa's trunk. There weren't many because most of the gifts had been stored in Ed's basement. Lisa and Jonathan had wrapped them and carried them up to the Christmas tree a few days earlier.

Jonathan stood in front of a full-length mirror and stared at his clothes. He was wearing the same pants he'd worn the night before, but he'd borrowed one of Ed's polo shirts. It was white with small emblem on the chest pocket. It was also larger than his normal size and it hung off his shoulders. "I hope Noah doesn't recognize your shirt," he said. "But I like wearing it. It feels sexy."

Ed grabbed his ass on the way out the door and said, "He won't notice. I'm going to down to make coffee. I'll tell them you came early and you're checking a few things out for the show in the other bathroom." Before he left, he unzipped his pants and spread the opening apart. "I like wearing your underwear, too," he said. While Jonathan had been looking for clean sheets, Ed had been putting on Jonathan's white briefs.

"You're wearing my underwear?" Jonathan asked. "I was looking for them this morning. I thought you'd put them in the hamper." Then he pulled down his zipper and said, "I'm wearing your boxers. But they are clean. I found them in your drawer."

Ed stared at Jonathan's crotch and licked his lips. "My way is sexier."

Jonathan pulled up his zipper and looked in the mirror again. "I just hope they don't recognize the shirt."

Ed waved his arm. "They won't."

But Lisa noticed right away. When Jonathan came down and walked into the kitchen, she was standing at the center island. She smiled and crossed the room to hug him and wish him a merry Christmas. She looked over his shoulder and smiled at Ed, then she pointed to the shirt Jonathan was wearing and silently mouthed the words, "Is this your shirt?"

Ed stepped back and gave her a look. Why on Earth would she think Jonathan was wearing his shirt? He pressed his lips together and stared down at the counter. He was making coffee, spooning the grounds into the coffee maker, trying not to spill any on the counter.

She threw her arms up in surrender and said, "You look so good this morning, Jonathan. So well rested." Then she smiled at Ed and stuck out her tongue.

Jonathan ignored her. "How's Noah doing? Did he mention Tucker at all this morning?" he asked.

Lisa frowned and said, "Are you kidding? He made me drive around the whole neighborhood for a half hour before we got here, looking for him. He didn't want me to mention it." She placed her palm on Ed's back. "He doesn't want his father to worry about him."

Ed closed the top of the coffee pot and pressed the switch. He ran his fingers through his hair and said, "Damn. Where is he now?"

"He's in the living room sitting in front of the Christmas tree," Lisa said. "He wanted to put a Christmas present under the tree for Tucker. It's a large dog sweater he bought when I took him shopping a few weeks ago. He wrapped it himself a few days before Tucker ran away."

"We should start opening presents soon," Ed said. "It will take his mind off it for a while."

When the coffee was finished, they went into the living room. Noah was sitting on the floor in front of the tree staring at one of the gifts. It wasn't wrapped very well and it wasn't in a box. The corners were crunched and the sides looked as if the wrapping paper had been rolled up and squeezed with tape. "What are you doing, buddy?" Ed asked.

"Nothing," Noah said. He stared down at the package and frowned.

"I thought we'd open our gifts right now," Ed said. "Help me bring a few chairs from the dining room in here so we have places to sit."

Noah stood up and walked through the room without saying a word. He went into the dining room and lifted a chair. It was the first time Ed noticed he was wearing a sweatshirt with Tucker's name across the front. Ed had bought it for him on the trip they'd taken to Hawaii last Christmas. He decided not the mention the shirt.

When the chairs were in the living room and it was time to open gifts, it seemed to take his mind off Tucker for a while. He gave Ed a new tool box and a nicely framed print of different dog breeds. He handed it to him and said, "Here, Dad. This is for when you open your new clinic in San Francisco for spaying and neutering dogs and cats."

Ed hugged him, then pointed to a large group of wrapped gifts on the left side of the tree. "Your gifts are over there, buddy," he said. Noah didn't believe in Santa Claus anymore. He'd asked Ed about it not long after Jake had been killed, and Ed had told him the truth. Ed had wanted to wait at least another year, but Noah had decided for him. Ed had a rule: when Noah asked him a question, he always told him the truth.

Noah's gifts from everyone were toys and other things a ten-year-old boy would like. When he was finished opening them, he thanked everyone and started handing out his gifts for the others.

He bought Jonathan a book about hot air balloons, because Jonathan had once expressed interest in the subject. He bought Lisa a bottle of perfume. Ed had taken him shopping for these things. Noah already knew she liked this perfume because she had an almost empty bottle on her dressing table.

When Ed handed Jonathan a small, thin, perfectly wrapped package, he said, "I hope you like this. Lisa mentioned you saw it at Gumps while you were both out shopping, so I went back and got it for you." Then he shrugged his shoulders and stared into the fireplace. "I hope it's okay."

Jonathan opened it fast. And when he saw that Ed had given him a first edition of *How the Grinch Stole Christmas*, he fell back in his seat. "This is too much, Ed. I never expected anything like this. I know how much it cost. I don't know what to say." He pressed on hand to his throat and smiled. "I'm stunned."

Ed shrugged. "Just say thank you, is all." He was uncomfortable with these warm, tender moments. But he was happy to see the thrilled expression on Jonathan's face. He'd wanted to make him happy with this gift. He would have paid twice as much if he'd had to.

Jonathan looked him in the eye. "I love it. And, yes, thank you."

The rest of the gifts were the typical sweaters and articles of clothing people usually exchange. But when it was time for Jonathan to give his gifts to Ed, no one expected a surprise gift. He gave Ed the black leather sport jacket first, and Ed smiled and thanked him. It turned out to be a perfect fit, and he liked the way it felt. Then Jonathan pulled another gift out from the back of the tree and said, "I thought you might like this, too." It was a large, heavy rectangle, wrapped with the same gold paper and red ribbon he'd used to wrap the sex toy.

Lisa stood up and put her hands on her hips. "Hey, no fair," she shouted. "You didn't tell me about this one, and we went shopping together."

Jonathan smiled and said, "I thought about this at the last minute, and forgot about it."

Ed took the gift and lifted it up and down. "It feels like wood," he said. He couldn't even begin to imagine what it was.

He held it on his lap and opened it slowly. His eyebrows wrinkled and his lips tightened. When all the paper was off, he sat there staring at it for a moment. It was a sign for above the front door with the name of the house, *Mi Casa de mis Sueños*. The background color was the same pale blue-green as the trim on the house in the Hamptons and the lettering was done in real gilt. He smiled and said, "This is perfect. I can't believe how perfect it is. I've been staring at the outside of the house wondering what's missing. And this is it." Then he rubbed his jaw and smiled again. "I love this."

"Well, what is it?" Lisa asked. From where she was sitting, she could only see the back of a wooden plank with a hook at the top.

He lifted his eyes to Jonathan and said, "Thank you." Then he turned the plaque around so that Lisa and Noah could see it.

But just as Noah was about to say something about the color of the plaque, the doorbell rang. He jumped up from the floor and shouted, "It could be Tucker. Maybe someone found him." Then he ran out of the room and into the front hall.

Ed looked at Jonathan and lifted his eyebrows. They both stood up from their chairs and followed Noah to the front door. For a moment Ed's heart raced with excitement. Maybe it *was* about Tucker. Maybe someone had found him and brought him home on Christmas Day. Ed had placed ads in newspapers, he'd posted signs all over town with Tucker's photo, and he'd posted information about him in the Internet.

But when he reached the front door, he frowned and placed his hands on Noah's shoulders. There was a delivery man standing in the doorway, a tall thin guy in tight jeans. He was holding a large flower arrangement in one hand and a clipboard in the other. He said he had a delivery for Lisa and that he needed a signature. Noah turned and shuffled back to the living room with his head bowed. Jonathan followed him. Ed signed the clipboard, handed the delivery guy a tip, and took the flowers.

It was such a large arrangement it hid Ed's entire face. He had to carry it with both hands. There were red reds and pinks mixed with oranges and purples. There were three shades of blue and light yellows. Large exotic greens were layered with pale ferns. The silver bow at the bottom was bigger than both of Ed's hands put together. The flowery aroma filled the room and masked the smell of the Christmas tree within minutes. Ed slanted his head to the side so he could see Lisa and said, "These are for you." He wanted to be more animated, but he couldn't stop thinking about the look on Noah's face when he saw a delivery man standing at the door instead of Tucker.

Lisa stood and gaped at the flowers. Her mouth opened and she shrugged her shoulders. When she reached for the card to see who it was from, she smiled and shook her head. Then she read the card aloud: "Just wanted you to know I was thinking about you. Hope you have a great holiday. I'll call you…Joel."

"Good old Joel," Ed said. "I'm starting to like that guy a lot."

"They are beautiful," Jonathan said, "I've known Joel for a long time and I know for a fact he never sends anyone flowers. He must really like you, Lisa."

She was gazing at the flowers and smiling. "I'd better get them in water," she said.

"I'll get a large vase out of the garage," Ed said. He knew there were several in boxes. Jake had loved fresh flowers and he'd always placed them in large crystal vases. He looked at Noah and said, "Do you want to come out and help me, buddy? I'm not sure where to look."

Noah was on the floor playing with one of his computer games. "I'll be there in a minute," he said. "I want to put Tucker's bowls out on the front steps first…in case he comes back and he's hungry or thirsty."

Ed sighed and said, "Take your time, buddy."

Chapter Fourteen

The day before New Year's Eve, Jonathan received two inter-esting phone calls. He was just about to leave the hotel to shoot more scenes at Ed's house when his cell phone rang. He had been hoping to get over to Ed's earlier that morning. They hadn't been together since Christmas morning and Jonathan was horny. Noah had been around the house all week during the daytime filming and construction, and they'd been keeping him busy at night with mov-ies and restaurants to keep his mind off Tucker.

The first phone call was from Jonathan's producer in New York. He was calling to tell him that his show, *Dream Away*, had been canceled that week. The network wanted to go in a different direction, with new shows that focused on contests and high-ener-gy competitions with huge giveaway prizes. They wanted a show with a higher profile that they could promote aggressively. The producer said they wanted to talk to Jonathan about a new show as soon as he finished shooting in San Francisco and returned to New York. He assured Jonathan that he wouldn't be out of a job and that even though *Dream Away* had been canceled, the network execu-tives still had plans for him. They liked him, they knew he brought ratings, and they wanted to keep him.

Jonathan didn't reply. He wasn't sure about all this yet. *Dream Away* had always maintained a certain dignity, with respect to pure design and architectural integrity. Jonathan didn't want to wind up on a new show that was advertised as "wacky and wild."

He didn't even have time to process the news, because the second call came a minute after he hung up with his producer. It was Mike calling from New York. He was back in the United States for a meeting and he was flying out to San Francisco that night to spend New Year's Eve with Jonathan. Mike didn't ask if he could come. He didn't even ask how Jonathan was. Mike just told him when he'd be arriving in that no-nonsense, businesslike tone of voice he used with everyone. Then he said, "I feel like it's been years since I've been able to hold you in my arms, beloved. I can't wait for us to be together again, my love."

Jonathan frowned and pressed his palm against his forehead. This was a perfect example of the way Mike had always tried to control him. They weren't committed to each other and Mike knew it. First he spoke to him like he was an employee. Then he spoke in that cheesy, overly dramatic way that turned Jonathan's stomach into knots. Who said "beloved"?

So Jonathan told him he already had plans for New Year's Eve and that he couldn't get out of them. He wasn't lying. He told Mike he'd been invited to Frank's and Greg's house, along with Ed, Lisa, and Noah, for a small house party. "You should have called earlier," Jonathan said. "I've already made a commitment and I can't very well say no now. Maybe you should just stay in New York."

But that didn't stop Mike. This was just a small inconvenience to him. "I'm coming anyway. I already have my ticket. I'm sure they won't mind if you bring a friend along to this sweet little party. Now I have to run. I'm late for a meeting downtown. I'll call you when I arrive in San Francisco."

Jonathan tried to stop him, but he hung up so fast they didn't even say goodbye. This was another one of Mike's control tactics. He believed that if he pursued anything long enough, he'd get what he wanted. Jonathan also picked up on his comment referring to the "sweet little party." This was Mike's passive aggressive way of showing his superiority...only he did it with a slight lisp and "sweet" sounded like "thweet."

When Jonathan walked into Ed's house a few minutes later, Ed was in the kitchen sipping a cup of coffee and eating toast. There were crumbs all over the new granite counter next to the refrigerator and he'd left the butter out at room temperature uncovered. It was still early. No one else had arrived yet, and Noah was probably just waking up over at the guest house so they had at last a half hour to talk.

Jonathan looked at the crumbs and the butter and shook his

head. Ed could be a real slob sometimes. Normally, this wouldn't have bothered him. But that morning it made the short hairs on the back of his neck stand up. "You should cover the butter," Jonathan said, "You can get sick that way. It's not sanitary."

Ed put down his coffee and walked over to him. He put one arm around Jonathan's shoulder and grabbed his ass with his other hand. He kissed him on the mouth and said, "Let's go upstairs." Then Ed grabbed his own crotch and shook it up and down a few times. He was still in his bare feet and he was wearing his camouflage shorts and a white T-shirt. "All you have to do is drop your pants and bend over the bed. I'll do all the work."

Jonathan sighed and licked his neck. He looked cute in his bare feet. Ed hadn't shaved and the rough stubble pricked his tongue and sent blood rushing to his penis. But he pulled away and said, "I have to tell you something first." He wasn't going to mention the show being canceled right away. He still wanted to think about that for a while.

"What?"

"I just got a call from Mike," Jonathan said. "He's in New York for a few days and he's coming out here late tonight. He wants to spend New Year's Eve with me."

Ed rubbed his jaw a few times and stared at the counter. "Is this the same Mike you were dating in New York for a while? The one who gave you that watch?"

Jonathan nodded yes. "But we're not committed and we're not a couple. I never made future plans with him, and I didn't ask him to come out here." He suddenly felt the need to defend himself, though he hadn't done anything wrong.

"Did you tell him you have plans for New Year's?" Ed asked. His fists were clenched now and a small vein in his neck throbbed.

"Of course I did," Jonathan said. "He insisted on coming anyway. This is how Mike is. He's a pit bull. When he sinks his teeth into something, he never lets go."

"You could have told him not to come," Ed said.

"I tried," Jonathan said, "but he wouldn't listen. Mike is like that. He's used to getting whatever he wants."

"Are you going to *fuck* him when he's here?" Ed asked. It came out fast and his voice went lower than usual. "Are you going to *suck* Mike's dick like you suck mine?"

Jonathan's face dropped and his body froze. He clenched his own his fists and said, "I can't believe you'd say something like that to me. I thought you were different. I guess I was wrong about you after all." He turned to leave and said, "Tell the crew to shoot without me today. Tell them I have a weird stomach flu and I'll be back to work the January second. I really need to get out of here right now."

Then he left Ed standing alone in the kitchen and crossed to the front hallway. He squared his shoulders and lifted his head. His lips were on the verge of trembling and tears were forming at the corners of his eyes, but he didn't want Ed to see how hurt he was. He heard the sound of his own heels clicking against the wooden floors and his heart pounded in his chest.

When he reached for the doorknob, a strong hand grabbed his arm and pulled it back. "Don't leave," Ed said. "I'm sorry. I didn't mean that. It's just that this guy Mike makes me crazy. He's only coming out here for one reason."

Jonathan tried to pull away, but Ed was a strong man. "Let go of me," Jonathan said. "You're hurting my arm." Ed wasn't really hurting his arm, but Jonathan wanted him to think he was.

Ed wrapped his other hand around his waist and pulled him away from the door. "Why didn't you tell Mike about *us*? He should fucking know about me. I deserve that."

Jonathan's eyes opened wide and his head went back. He looked into Ed's eyes and said, "What should I tell him about us? We haven't made any commitments to each other. At least not as far as I know. Please let me know if I've missed something, Ed. You won't even tell Noah or Lisa about us. And you know damn well I'd never say anything because I love Noah and I don't want to confuse him."

Ed tightened his grip. "Stop acting like a child. You're having a temper tantrum."

Suddenly, Jonathan was tired of being controlled by everyone. The television network was trying to control his career, Mike had been controlling his personal life, and now Ed was trying to do the same thing to him. "Let go of me, Ed."

"Let's go into the kitchen and talk about this rationally," Ed said. "Calm down." Ed leaned forward and his legs were bent. He put his other arm around Jonathan's waist and held him even tighter.

Jonathan's heart beat fast and his eyes bulged. He shouted, "I don't want to talk about it. Let go of me. I want to be alone for a while. I'm going to fly back to New York today and spend New Year's all alone in my own apartment."

Then Ed turned him around, lifted him off the ground and threw him over his shoulders. He carried him back to the kitchen. Jonathan kicked his legs and pounded his fists on Ed's back. But he wasn't pounding hard. He didn't want to hurt him.

When they reached the kitchen, Ed stretched out his right arm and cleared the top of the center island with one quick swipe. Newspapers fell to the floor, the salt and pepper grinders landed under the table on the other side of the room, and Ed's coffee cup cracked into pieces next to the island. He was still holding

Jonathan over his shoulder with the other arm, and Jonathan was still kicking his legs.

"What are you doing, Ed?" Jonathan shouted. "Have you lost your mind? Put me down, you big *idiot*."

Ed lowered Jonathan to the counter and wrapped his arms around Jonathan's body. He pressed the right side of his face to Jonathan's chest and said, "I think I have lost my mind. I've lost it for you. Don't leave. Let's just talk this out like rational adults. I'm am a big idiot sometimes, but I don't want you to leave like this." Ed didn't sob, but there were tears in his eyes and he sniffed back a few times.

Jonathan stopped fighting; his body relaxed. He cupped Ed's head in his palms and lifted it to his face. He looked into his wet eyes and said, "I'm not going anywhere." He kissed his forehead and swallowed hard. "And you're not an idiot. You're a fantastic man and a very good father."

Ed stared at Jonathan for a second, then grabbed the back of his head and kissed him hard. Jonathan shoved his tongue into Ed's mouth and held his shoulders. Then he ran his palms across the large muscles on Ed's back and rolled his tongue in circles. Ed tasted like a man should taste. The wiry stubble on his face burned and scratched Jonathan's skin. He knew he couldn't fight back anymore, because this was the one rare exception when he needed to be controlled.

When Ed finally pulled him off the counter, he turned him around and said, "Pull down your pants." Then he yanked down his zipper and pulled out his erection. He leaned into Jonathan and started to dry hump his leg with hard pounds. "I need you now."

Jonathan bit the inside of his mouth and clutched the counter. No one had ever dry humped him before. He knew Ed wanted to fuck him right there in the kitchen. "What if someone comes in?" Jonathan whispered. He leaned back, slanted his head, and kissed Ed's chin.

"I don't fucking care anymore," Ed said. "Now pull down your pants and lean over the counter."

While Jonathan lowered his jeans, Ed reached for the butter on the counter behind them. It was unsalted, whipped butter in a round container. He stuck two fingers into the container and rubbed the soft white butter all over his dick. "Open your legs," Ed said. He spread the butter around the lips of Jonathan's hole and covered it until it was slick and ready for entry.

Ed mounted him hard. It reminded Jonathan of the first few times they'd had sex. The heavy breathing, the racing hearts, the dripping sweat brought it all back. And there was nothing awkward or forced about it. Ed's thick erection penetrated Jonathan's tight hole as if it had been sized for a custom fit. Ed bucked his hips with vicious thrusts and rammed his cock to the bottom of Jonathan's ass with brunt force. Jonathan arched his back and gripped the other side of the counter for support. He held his own erection and jerked to the rhythm of Ed's fucking. With each loud slam and crack, he came closer to a release.

A few minutes later, Ed slapped his ass hard and filled his hole with come. Jonathan came at the same time and shot all over the kitchen cabinets. When it was over, Ed kissed the back of his neck and asked, "Are you okay now?"

Jonathan knew he wasn't talking about his physical condition. He was talking about his emotional state. So he backed into Ed, rotated his hips around a few times, and said, "I'm good."

"Are we okay?" Ed asked. He was still inside and his hands were massaging Jonathan's ass cheeks.

"We're good," Jonathan said. "But you'd better pull out now so I can go upstairs and clean up fast. The crew will be here at any minute and I feel buttery and grimy."

Ed laughed and gave him one last pound. Then he slapped his ass again and said, "Yeah, you'd better wash all that butter off your butt. It's not sanitary."

Chapter Fifteen

When Mike called Jonathan from the airport on New Year's Eve, Jonathan, Ed, and Noah were downtown looking at an empty storefront in the Lower Haight section of the city. Ed had read the advertisement in the newspaper. The storefront was actually on Haight Street, not far from Fillmore. It was the sort of neighborhood where you'd expect to see bars and lounges instead of a low-cost veterinary clinic that focused on neutering and spaying animals. But it was exactly the sort of place Ed had been picturing in his mind: less commercial than Upper Haight, with a mixed variety of essentials that ranged from an elementary school to a Zen center. He wasn't doing this to make a profit. He already had more money than he'd ever be able to spend in his lifetime. He wanted this to be a community service.

It was after five o'clock in the afternoon and they were walking back to the car. Ed was wearing the new black leather sport jacket Jonathan had given him for Christmas. The weather was cool. It was one of those sunny and crisp San Francisco days between winter rain storms. Jonathan's cell phone rang and he reached into his back pocket to answer it. Ed had just unlocked the car and was opening the back door for Noah. Jonathan turned away from them

189

so they couldn't hear what he was saying. He spoke for all of two minutes, then closed his phone and put it back in his pocket. His jeans were tight, so he had to force the phone into his pants.

Ed smiled and asked, "Who was that?" He already knew, but he didn't want to look jealous. He wondered why Jonathan was wearing those tight low-rise jeans. They were the ones that made his ass round out and bubble. He could have worn the baggy tan pants that made his ass look flat.

Jonathan shrugged his shoulders and checked to see that Noah's door was secured. He stared down at the handle and said, "It was Mike. He's at the airport. You'll have to drop me off at the hotel so I can go get him. He said it was silly for him to rent a car when I already have one."

Ed opened the driver's door and said, "We'll just go now. I don't mind driving you over." He looked into the back seat and said to Noah. "We're going to the airport to pick up Jonathan's old buddy from New York, Mike." He was smiling and his voice was calm. But he spoke with an over-animated tone that bordered the thin line between sarcasm and arrogance.

"I don't want you to go out of your way, Ed," Jonathan said, crossing to the other side of the car. "It might be better if I just get him and bring him to the party later tonight."

He knew he could take advantage of the situation because

Noah was listening, so he waved his arm and said, "I can't wait to meet this Mike. Don't give it a second thought."

But the drive to the airport was quiet. The only one who spoke at all was Noah. He was excited about Ed's new clinic. He liked the location they'd just seen and he was hoping his father would rent it. Ed said he had a good feeling about it, too, and said he was going to call the landlord and put down a deposit. When Ed asked Jonathan for his opinion, Jonathan looked him in the eye and said, "I think it's the best thing you've decided to do since you've moved here."

When they arrived at the airport, Mike was standing outside the terminal waiting for them. Jonathan pointed to a tall man with blond hair near an airport limousine. He was standing beside a set of pretentious designer luggage, with a matching bag over his shoulder. He wore a pale blue, button-down oxford, loafers and cream-colored slacks. Jonathan said, "That's him over there, the guy with the blond hair and the Gucci bags."

Ed rubbed his jaw. "You mean the one with the pink sweater over his shoulders with the sleeves tied together?" He didn't smile, but he was making fun of him.

Jonathan glared at him. "Yes," he said.

"If he's only staying one night, why does he have so much luggage?" Ed asked. He'd counted three suitcases plus the shoulder bag. Ed had met *his* kind before: a pretentious New York queen who came from nothing, got lucky, and pretended he was old money for the rest of his life.

"Mike packs for everything," Jonathan said, shrugging his shoulders.

Ed tapped the Range Rover's horn a few times and pulled up to the curb. Jonathan got out of the car, went to Mike, and hugged him. It was only a quick, harmless hug, but Ed clenched his teeth and frowned. Then he got out of the car and opened the back hatch so they could load Mike's luggage. He forced himself to smile. He didn't want to resort to junior high school drama.

When Jonathan introduced Mike to Ed, Ed's eyebrows immediately rose and his head slanted to the right. Mike leaned forward and bent his knees as if he were about to curtsy—it was an almost-curtsy—and said, "It's lovely to meet you, Ed." Then he extended his right arm forward, palm down, as if he expected Ed to kiss his hand.

What the fuck?

Ed wasn't sure what to do, so he grabbed Mike's limp fingers and shook them a couple of times. He certainly wasn't going to kiss his hand. "It's nice to meet you, too, buddy," Ed said. Then he turned to Jonathan and said, "Jonathan's told me so much about you." In fact, Jonathan had barely mentioned Mike. Ed was still smiling, but his back teeth were bonded together.

On the way to the hotel, Mike sat in the back seat with Noah behind Jonathan. Mike did most of the talking. He complained about the flight, trashed the flight attendants, and ranted endlessly about the senile fat woman who had been sitting next to him on the plane. Noah's eyes grew large, but he didn't speak. "It was like sitting with Aunt Clara from *Bewitched* for over six hours," Mike said.

Mike wasn't outrageously flamboyant, but he had noticeable effeminate qualities. The way he sat with his knees together and his feet crossed at the ankle; he waved his arm and his hand wobbled at the wrist. Ed kept looking back at him in the rearview mirror, wondering if his blond hair was natural. When he said the word "rather," he used a pretentious accent and it sounded like "rah-thah." Ed rubbed his jaw and creased his eyebrows while he drove, trying to imagine what this guy and Jonathan could possibly have in common.

Halfway there, Mike ran his hand across the back of Jonathan's leather seat and said, "You have a *lovely* car, Ed. I was going to buy a Range Rover, but I heard there were problems with the suspension. So I bought a Porsche Cayenne instead."

"Ah well," Ed said. "I don't have any complaints about the Range Rover. It's rugged and sturdy. A real man's car." He made a fist and pounded the arm rest on the center console. He wanted to spit out the window and belch, but he didn't want to upset Jonathan.

"I see," Mike said. Then he folded his hands and rested them on his knees.

Ed caught Jonathan rolling his eyes. Noah's mouth dropped open as he stared at Mike's clear nail polish.

When they finally reached the hotel, Noah tapped Ed on the shoulder and said, "Can I stay with Jonathan, Dad? I've never seen his hotel room."

Ed smiled. He felt like reaching back and hugging his son. He wished he'd been clever enough to think of this on his own. He'd been wondering about leaving Jonathan alone with Mike. The thought of them in a hotel room made his stomach churn. Jonathan had already assured Ed that they had separate rooms—Mike preferred to sleep alone—but he had a feeling Mike would try to get into Jonathan's pants before the party. So Ed told Noah, "Of course you can stay, buddy. As long as it's okay with Jonathan." Then Ed looked at Jonathan with his most innocent expression and shrugged his shoulders.

Jonathan gave him a look. He seemed to know what Ed was doing. "Sure he can stay. I'll just bring him with us to the party in a few hours. We'll meet you there."

"Ah well, I guess I can take a short nap then," Mike said. But he wasn't smiling.

It was a good thing the party was casual and Noah didn't have to change his clothes, because they didn't show up until after eight o'clock. Ed and Lisa arrived at seven o'clock, then Ed paced the living room floor for more than an hour waiting for them. At first he was worried about Mike and Jonathan, but then he started to worry about Noah.

When they finally arrived, Ed pulled Jonathan aside and asked, "Where were you? I was ready to call the police."

Jonathan shrugged. "Noah and I were ready to leave at seven, but Mike took a nap, a long hot bath, and then he couldn't decide between the lime green jacket or the faux fur sweater. We sat in my hotel room waiting for him for over an hour."

Ed turned his head in Mike's direction. Lisa was introducing him to Frank and Greg. Mike was wearing a black sweater with brown, fake fur trim that ran down the front in two straight lines. His right arm was stretched out, palm down, and he was doing the almost-curtsy thing again. "He should have gone with the lime jacket," Ed said, "because the sweater was a mistake."

Jonathan kissed him on the cheek and said, "Be nice, and stop worrying. You have nothing to be jealous about. I'm going to talk to him before he leaves and tell him we're finished. I've been thinking about it for a long time." Then he went into the kitchen to help Lisa and Frank set up a small buffet table in the dining room.

But Ed wasn't thoroughly convinced of that yet. If Mike could be persuasive enough to attract Jonathan once, he could always do it again. So he volunteered to be the bartender that night. He told Frank and Greg that he wanted to help out because they were so busy organizing the food. And when Mike quietly asked for a club soda with a twist of lime, Ed slapped his back playfully and insisted on making him a special drink. "It's something you'll love, buddy," Ed told him.

A few minutes later, Ed handed him an amber-colored drink in a tall crystal glass and said, "Drink up, buddy." It was his version of a Long Island Iced Tea, which was all booze with two small ice cubes. Ed had learned how to make it one summer when he'd worked part time as a bartender in college. His version tasted even more like real iced tea, without a hint of the taste of alcohol.

Mike took it from him and sipped from the edge of the glass with his pinky finger extended. His lips smacked a few times and he looked surprised. "That's very tasty, indeed. Thank you."

"Drink up, buddy," Ed said. "There's plenty more."

In spite of Mike, it turned out to be a nice party. The food was good, they played a few games, and Noah seemed to forget about Tucker for a few hours. Ed kept giving Mike refills, and Mike kept drinking them down as if he were drinking ice water. He didn't seem drunk at all. The alcohol seemed to relax him. His voice became more animated and he stopped sitting with his knees clamped together. When he started bonding with Frank and Greg, he didn't even notice anymore that Jonathan was in the room.

Mike sat in the middle of one sofa most of the night holding court. Frank sat on his right and Greg was on his left. When Mike told them he collected vintage cars, he batted his eyelashes at Frank and ran his fingers along Greg's arm. When he said he owned a 1972 AMC Hornet and a 1973 AMC Gremlin, they pretended to be fascinated. Greg leaned in closer and stared at his lips and Frank squeezed his thigh. Mike blushed and said he'd even named his Hornet and Gremlin after characters in the old Bette Davis movie, *Whatever Happened to Baby Jane?* The Hornet was Blanche Hudson and the Gremlin was Jane Hudson.

While Lisa, Jonathan, and Noah played a board game on the other side of the room, Ed sat alone in a club chair and listened to Mike talk about his cars. The more he drank, the longer he talked. Ed rested his chin in his palm and pretended to be interested, but for the life of him he couldn't understand why anyone would want to collect old AMC cars, especially a Hornet and a Gremlin. In Ed's opinion, they were two of the most God-awful, ugly cars ever produced in America. He remembered a mean aunt on his mother's side who had a Gremlin. She also had hair on her upper lip and a mole on her chin; she always wore navy blue skirts like an ex-nun. She drove that hideous old car until she died in 1988. If Ed were going to collect old cars, it would have been something strong and important, like an old Cadillac or Lincoln. Or one of those cool, old pickup trucks with wood from the 1940s. He couldn't picture Jonathan sitting behind the wheel of an old AMC car. But he could see Mike driving one, wearing pink lipstick with matching pink sunglasses.

By the time Ryan Seacrest counted down to the New Year on television, the party started to wind down as well. Ed, Lisa, and Jonathan kissed each other and said, "Happy New Year!" then Jonathan got up to use the powder room. Noah was sleeping on another sofa near the TV. He'd tried to stay up until midnight, but he'd started drifting off around eleven.

So Ed decided to carry him over to the guest house and put him to bed. Lisa was ready to leave, too. Ed told her he'd stay with Noah in the guest house alone, but she pulled him to the side and said, "I think it's time to go now." Then she nodded at Mike. He was still on the sofa with Frank and Greg. They didn't even know it was after midnight. Mike's eyes were red, his voice was slurred, and he kept laughing for no reason at all. Greg had his hand on Mike's thigh and Frank was massaging his shoulders. There had been signs all night, but now it was obvious they were trying to get into Mike's pants.

Ed smiled. "Interesting," he said. "Let's get Noah to bed." They weren't doing anything offensive, but he didn't want Noah exposed to something he wouldn't understand.

Lisa punched him in the arm. "You love it and you know it," she said. "I saw the way you were pouring Mike drinks all night. I'm surprised he hasn't passed out yet."

Ed shrugged. "I wanted him to have fun. But I honestly didn't expect this to happen." He was telling the truth. He thought he'd just get him too drunk to do anything with Jonathan. He never expected Frank and Greg to lure him into their bed as a third.

She laughed and leaned closer. "Oh, he will have fun. I know for a fact that both Frank and Greg are top guys in bed. They told me so. And they love three-ways."

Jonathan came out of the powder room and saw Ed and Lisa talking. He looked at the other side of the room and raised an eyebrow. He crossed to the sofa where Lisa and Ed were standing and said, "I'll carry Noah to the guest house."

"I was just going to do that," Ed said. "I thought you might want to stay here a little longer and enjoy the party with old Mike." He was teasing him.

Jonathan smirked, and with a sarcastic tone he said, "You'd

better let me carry Noah. I'm younger than you are. I don't want you to hurt your back, old buddy." Then he bent down, put his arms under Noah's body, and lifted him slowly off the sofa.

Ed turned his head to the sofa on the other side of the room. Frank and Greg were gazing at Mike, and Mike's eyelids fluttered. "Should we say we're leaving?" Ed asked.

"We'll call them in the morning and thank them for the party," Lisa said. "Trust me, I know these guys. They won't be upset if we just leave quietly."

Chapter Sixteen

On the first day of March, Ed threw a party in the newly renovated house. It was a warm, dry day and typical of San Francisco's pleasant springtime weather. Noah was turning eleven years old. Jonathan had suggested to Ed a few weeks earlier that having a large birthday party for Noah would also be a great way to celebrate the end of the renovation.

This was a Saturday, and the film crew was wrapping up with one final shoot in the middle of the week to show the finished house. When it aired in the fall, it would be the final episode of *Dream Away*.

The house looked good. The walls had been painted white, the old wooden floors had been refinished with a dark stain, and the kitchen and all the bathrooms were brand new. The furniture and artwork had been delivered and everything was perfect. Ed had been firm about maintaining as much of the original architecture as possible so the integrity of the house would not be compromised, and he'd been correct. With the help of an excellent contractor and a dedicated crew, he'd managed to bring both the exterior and interior of the house back to its original glory in a relatively short amount of time.

Along with Noah's school friends, everyone involved with the renovation attended the party. Ed had asked Jonathan to make up a guest list, and Jonathan had invited them all, including his own film crew from the television network. He'd even invited Frank and Greg. He hadn't seen much of them since New Year's Eve, but Lisa and Noah were still talked to them daily. Greg had been calling Jonathan for two weeks about a possible job at the TV station in San Francisco where he worked. Jonathan had been planning to get back to him sooner, but wrapping up the show and dealing with the party had taken up most of his time. He wanted this party to be special, a day that would make Noah smile for years to come. The poor kid hadn't been the same since Tucker had disappeared, and Jonathan hated the thought of leaving him and going back to New York without giving him something wonderful to remember. Jonathan knew they would always be friends, but he wasn't sure if his relationship with Ed would ever go beyond what it was.

Jonathan had spoken with the network executives in February. They wanted him to sign a three-year contract for a new television show for twice the amount he was getting paid now. The new show would begin taping in May. They wanted him to host a home renovation show that focused on second marriages where the couples were starting over. The twist to this show, tentatively titled, *Robbing the Cradle*, was that all the men would be at least twenty-five years older than the women. It was all about young women and older men starting new families and designing new homes. The women would all be young, blond, and gorgeous, and the men would all be distinguished, wealthy, and on their second or third marriages. When they pitched it to him, Jonathan shook his head and smiled, then told them he'd talk about it when he returned to New York. Evidently, the network was going for ratings with a younger crowd this time, because Jonathan had a feeling a lot of middle-aged first wives wouldn't be watching.

The money they offered him was great, he'd get a great deal of exposure, and the fact that they wanted him so badly was flattering. But if he took this job, he knew he'd be drifting even father away from his original career objective of becoming a serious journalist. The fact that *Robbing the Cradle* sounded like such a sleazy show could actually ruin his career altogether. For the first time in a long time, Jonathan wasn't sure about anything.

He didn't mention any of this to Ed. They were still going strong in bed, but Ed never talked about the future. After Jonathan officially broke up with Mike on New Year's Day, he thought Ed might want to take their relationship to another level. But Ed never said a word, and Jonathan wasn't going to force him into anything he wasn't ready to handle.

The only new face at the party was a young woman named

Katie. Ed had begun his venture with the animal clinic in Lower Haight and he'd hired her as his assistant. She was a full-time animal science teacher at a local college. She'd be working part time with Ed at the clinic during the school year and full time in the summers. Katie had long, brown hair, an hourglass figure, and the kind of no-nonsense personality that could make the meanest pit bull back down. She was good for Ed; she'd keep him organized. And Noah couldn't stop staring at the low-cut blouses she wore.

Everyone was laughing and the stereo was playing Linda Eder. Jonathan was standing under a rented tent in the back garden watching Noah when Greg walked up to his side and asked, "Can we talk for a minute?"

"Sure," Jonathan said, "I'm sorry I didn't get back to you, but I've been so busy with the party and everything I didn't have a chance." Actually, he'd been avoiding him on purpose ever since Mike had done a three-way with them. Jonathan didn't really care, but he wasn't sure how Frank and Greg felt about it.

Greg smiled. "Don't worry about it. I figured I'd talk to you today," he said. He didn't waste any time. "There's an opening at the station for a new co-anchor for the evening news. I remember you'd said your real passion was journalism. I figured I'd ask."

Jonathan's head slanted to the side and he furrowed his eyebrows. "Are you offering me a job doing the news?"

Greg shrugged. Then he smiled and said, "Are you interested? I think you'd be a great addition to the entire news team. I've even talked about it with everyone, and they agree with me. We can talk about the details later."

Jonathan thought for a moment. A job like that would probably mean less money and much less national exposure. But at least he'd be doing what he loved to do. It would also mean relocating, and he wasn't sure about that either. "Well, thank you. Can I let you know early this week?"

Greg laughed and slapped him on the back. "Hell, yes. I thought you'd blow me off politely. Take your time to think about it and call me when you're ready to talk. But I *will* need someone by the end of the month." Then he hugged him and went back to where Frank was standing.

Ed came up to Jonathan's side and asked, "What were you talking about with Greg?"

He smelled like aftershave. Jonathan took a deep breath and said, "The weather." It was none of Ed's business. If he took the job in San Francisco, which he wasn't sure he was going to do, he didn't want to be influenced by Ed.

Ed sulked. "You did a great job with the party. They're having a blast." He was drinking beer from a bottle. His white shirt had a few wrinkles near the collar and he'd forgotten to shave that morning. But he looked good in his olive slacks. They were the tight ones that bunched up between his legs and made his crotch look huge.

"I think Noah's enjoying himself," Jonathan said. He watched Noah and a few kids from school eat birthday cake. Noah was smiling and there was white frosting on the left side of his face. One of the camera men was filming him. Jonathan had asked if they could get a few shots of the party for the final episode of the TV show.

"I just hope he likes what I got him for his birthday," Ed said. He placed the empty bottle of beer on a table beside Jonathan. When he brought his hand back, he purposely rubbed it against Jonathan's ass.

Jonathan continued staring at Noah. "Be good," he said. "Didn't you get enough this morning?" Jonathan had spent the night, and he'd opened his eyes in the morning with Ed's erection pressed to his lips. Even though he had been wondering about their relationship and where it would go after the film crew packed up and went home, he couldn't say no to sex with Ed. And it wasn't just because he wanted to please him. Jonathan enjoyed it too much to say no.

Ed shrugged. "I guess not. We should sneak into the bushes when no one's looking and you should take off your clothes for me." He had a serious expression, as if he were talking about a business deal instead of getting into Jonathan's pants.

Jonathan smiled and ignored the comment. "What did you get Noah?"

"A new puppy," he said. "Katie does a lot of part-time rescue work at the shelter and she found a black lab puppy this week. A family bought him at a pet shop without understanding what's involved with raising a puppy and put him up for adoption. We're hiding him upstairs until it's time to open the gifts. I haven't told anyone. You're the only one who knows. Do you think I did the right thing?"

Jonathan turned and looked into Ed's eyes. He knew Ed meant well, but he had a feeling Noah wouldn't be jumping for joy. He was still grieving for Tucker. But Jonathan smiled and said, "I think you're a wonderful father."

When it was time for Noah to open his gifts, Ed went into the house to get the new puppy. There weren't really that many gifts, because Jonathan had made it clear to the construction crew and the film crew that they were not required to bring anything. Most of the gifts were small items from Noah's classmates. And Frank and Greg handed him a huge card with a note inside that read, "Surprise Birthday Present: March 2, at One p.m.." Then there was a Sonoma County address in small print at the bottom.

Noah smiled and asked. "What is this?"

Greg lifted his eyebrows and said, "It's a surprise. Frank and I wanted to get you something we knew you'd really love. You'll find out tomorrow. We're picking everyone up tomorrow and we're all going there together."

Frank stood next to Greg. His shoulders were squared and his arms were folded across his chest. His entire face was beaming with pride. "We've become very fond of you, Noah." Then he turned to Lisa and Jonathan and said, "We wanted to do something really special. This is sort of a birthday present and going away present for Lisa." Then he hugged Lisa and said, "We're really going to miss her when she goes back to New York at the end of the week."

Lisa started to cry. She was going home for good and she seemed excited about seeing Joel again, but she'd miss them all. "I'll be back a lot, and you guys can come to New York, too."

Noah stood up and thanked them both. And while he was hugging Greg, he looked at the patio door and his mouth fell open. A sharp, high-pitched yelp came from the house and everyone turned to see what it was. Ed was loping toward them, carrying a hefty black puppy in his arms. The puppy was licking his face and his tail was wagging so fast it was hitting Ed's shoulder.

Ed shouted, "Happy birthday, buddy." Then he crossed to

where Noah was standing and placed the puppy on the grass next to him.

The puppy moved fast. He jumped up and licked Noah's face; his powerful tail knocked a martini glass off a table, then his hindquarters knocked the table over. Noah stepped back and wiped his face with the side of his hand, then he gazed down at the puppy with a blank stare.

"Isn't he great, Noah?" Ed said. "He's a rescue. Katie found him a few days ago and I knew he was perfect."

Noah patted the puppy's head a couple of times and said, "Thanks, Dad. It's a great present." But he wasn't smiling; he didn't even bend down to hug the new puppy. He just looked at Ed and asked, "Can I go play with my friends now?"

The corners of Ed's lips went down and his arms went limp at his sides. "Sure you can," he said.

Jonathan's eyes narrowed and he wanted to hug Ed right there in front of everyone. His intentions had been so good, and now he looked so lost standing there. But Noah wasn't ready to replace Tucker. He couldn't help the way he felt. Jonathan was about to say something to make Ed feel better, but his cell phone started to vibrate in his back pocket. He normally would have turned the phone off, but he was waiting for a call about extending his rental car a few more days. The rental company had made a mistake and

Jonathan was trying to clear it up.

He stepped back and turned to face the house. But when he answered the phone it wasn't the rental car company. It was a woman calling about a lost dog that matched Tucker's description. They'd placed Jonathan's cell phone number on the fliers they'd posted all over town just in case. Noah had been afraid Ed might miss a call. He tended to ignore his cell phone battery and it was always going dead.

When Jonathan hung up, he crossed back to where Ed was standing and grabbed his arm. "I just got a call about a dog that matched Tucker's description. The woman who called saw the flier. He's not wearing a collar, but it sounds just like him."

Ed rubbed his jaw a few times and frowned. "Should I tell Noah? If it's not Tucker, it could be traumatic for him."

Jonathan shrugged and smiled with his lips pressed together. "I'd want to know."

So they pulled Noah away from the party without telling anyone about this except Lisa. Ed asked her to watch the party and the new puppy, and Jonathan told Noah he wanted to show him something in the house. When Ed met them in the front hall, he said to Noah, "I don't know if it's true, but a woman just called and she thinks she has Tucker."

Noah's eyes doubled in size. "Where is he?"

"I have directions," Jonathan said. "We're going there right now. I'll get his leash and put it in the car."

* * * *

The woman who made the call lived outside the city on one of those hills that were stippled with homes overlooking the bay. When they pulled into the driveway, she was standing at the front door waiting for them. The house was a white, modern conglomerate of elegant cement cubes, with walls of glass surrounded by lush gardens. The woman's arms were folded across her chest and she was shaking her head back and forth. She looked like she was in her mid-fifties, with long red curls pulled back in a pony tail.

They all jumped out of the car and Ed asked, "Where is he?"

She frowned. "I tried to hold on to him, but he took off and ran out the back door," she said. "He tried to take off down the cliff, but he slipped and now he's trapped on a rock." She pointed to the rear of the house and took a deep breath. "He can't go up and he can't go down. He's trapped. It's very steep and very dangerous."

"I'm going back there," Ed said.

Jonathan grabbed his arm. "We're not even sure it's Tucker. Don't do anything foolish. We should call the police or the fire department." Jonathan knew Ed had a fear of heights and he didn't want to see him get hurt or lose his life by acting on impulse.

"I'm going back there now," Ed said. Then he took off and ran around the side of the house to the back yard.

Noah looked at Ed's back. He stretched his right arm and shouted, "Dad."

Then Jonathan, Noah, and the woman followed him. When they reached the back yard, Ed was standing at the edge of the property line. His hands were on his hips and he was smiling and shaking his head back and forth. He looked back at them and said, "It's him, all right. I don't know how he managed to get here, but it's definitely Tucker."

Jonathan took Noah's hand and they moved carefully to where Ed was standing. The woman followed not far behind, taking slow, calculated steps. When they reached a point where they could stand safely and look down, Jonathan saw Tucker standing on a flat rock. He wagged his tail and shook his head back and forth, but he looked much thinner and there were a few bruises on his left hind leg. His tongue was hanging out and he was gazing up at Ed. It was too steep for him to jump back up, and there was nothing but a severe, lethal drop to his rear that consisted of sharp rocks and wide tree trunks. Jonathan had never been afraid of heights. But looking down that deadly slope made his heart skip a few beats.

"Tucker," Noah shouted.

When the dog heard Noah's voice, he started to bark and wag his tail faster. But Jonathan grabbed Noah's arm and said, "Ed, we need to get help. It's too dangerous for you to go down there and get him."

Ed sucked in his bottom lip and took a deep breath. Then he clenched his fists and said, "I think I can do it. I can slide down, grab him under my arm, and pull him back up again. It won't be that difficult. You keep Noah back there and hold on to him."

"No," Jonathan said, "I want to help. Let me go down. I can do it."

Ed said, "I am going to do this. You're the one who said I'm still young enough to do anything. Just keep Noah from coming too close."

"At least let me hold onto you," Jonathan said. "Or we can tie a rope around you and secure it to a tree."

"I'm fine," Ed said. "Just stay back."

"Be careful, Dad," Noah shouted.

"I will, son," Ed said. "I'll be okay. I promise."

Then Ed went down on the grass so he could slide down the slope on his right side. He held the trunk of a thin tree with his left hand so he'd have support. The muscles in his strong arm tightened and bulged to the surface of his skin. He moved fast, with smooth, graceful motions, as if he'd been climbing rocks all his life. If he was experiencing fear, you wouldn't have known it from the strong, confident expression on his face. He focused on reaching for Tucker; he braced his right foot on a sturdy rock for added support. Then he slapped his thigh with his left hand and said, "Come on, Tucker. Come up here so I can grab you. I'll hold you, boy. You're safe."

Jonathan stood there holding his breath. He wanted to lunge forward and grab Ed's hand for extra support, but he didn't want to let go of Noah. He was holding him against his side. Noah was clutching his arm so hard, there were fingerprints on his flesh.

The woman who lived there just stood still. She had one hand over her mouth and the other pressed to her throat.

Then Tucker barked once and jumped up. He rested his front paws on Ed's hip and licked Ed's arm. And without hesitating for one second, Ed clenched his teeth and slipped his arm around the dog's body. He scooped Tucker up, grunted so hard his entire face turned red, and began pulling him up to safer ground.

When they were halfway to the grass, Jonathan let go of Noah and said, "Stay here and don't move." Then he went to where Ed was and got down on his knees. He slipped his hands under Ed's arm and pulled. With one heave, both Ed and the dog were on level ground again. Tucker jumped over Ed's body and ran to Noah. He knocked him to the ground and licked his face so hard Noah tumbled over and his legs went up in the air.

The woman's hands dropped to her side and she took a deep

breath. She walked to Noah and Tucker and said, "Oh, thank God."

Ed was lying on his back. His chest was heaving and his shirt was soaked with perspiration. Jonathan was sitting next to him with his legs stretched out. "Are you okay?" Jonathan asked.

Ed wiped his brow and said, "I think so."

"I thought you were afraid of heights," Jonathan said.

Ed laughed and glanced up at the clear blue sky. "I thought so, too. I usually can't even look down a flight of stairs, but for some reason it doesn't bother me anymore. I don't even mind looking down the slope now." Then he sat up and smoothed out his shirt. There were dark smudges and grass stains on the front and the back. "Thanks for helping out," he said.

Jonathan waved his arm. "I didn't do anything."

"You were there for Noah," he said. "And I appreciate that." Then he rubbed his face and looked over the tree tops toward the bay. "This is going to sound silly, but I've been dying to ask you something since Christmas. I keep forgetting about it."

"What's that?"

"How on Earth did you ever come up with the color of the house sign you had made, the one you gave me for Christmas? That is the exact color of the trim on my house in East Hampton, and it's not a color you see every day. It's called Waterbury Green and I keep extra cans of it on hand all the time."

Jonathan leaned forward and tipped his head. He didn't know this about Ed's house. When he'd had the sign made he'd looked up the paint color Waterbury Green, because he'd liked it so much when he'd seen it during his visit to Joel's rental house. He went through five different paint manufacturers before he actually found it. "I went to visit Joel one weekend in East Hampton before I came out here. He's renting a house there on Lilly Pond Lane with trim that color. It was an awful weekend I'd rather forget, but I loved the house and never forgot the color of the trim."

Ed's head jerked to the side and he laughed. "Well, there's only one house on Lilly Pond Lane with that color trim, and it's not Martha Stewart's. Jake didn't like the color of Martha's trim and he wanted to make a statement with Waterbury Green. The house was in Jake's family for years and I inherited it when he died." He stared down at his lap for a moment and smiled, then he lifted his head and said, "Go figure. I'm renting my house to *Joel*...your good buddy from college and Lisa's new boyfriend."

"It's a great house," Jonathan said. Then he made a mental note to call Joel and tell him that he was renting Ed's house, because after what he'd seen the night he'd been there, he wanted to make sure Joel left the house in perfection condition when the lease was up.

"I'm glad I didn't sell it," Ed said. "We may go back this summer."

Noah interrupted them. He was kneeling on the grass and his arms were wrapped around Tucker's neck. "We better go home now, Dad. So Tucker can meet the new puppy. I hope they like each other."

Ed rubbed his face with both hands and said, "I just realized I now have two dogs. I didn't plan on that."

Jonathan stood up and brushed off his jeans. He turned to face Noah and Tucker and said, "A lot of people have two dogs and they do just fine. I'd have a dozen if I could." Then he crossed back to the front of the house so he could get Tucker's leash from the car. He had a feeling Ed was watching him walk away.

Chapter Seventeen

Ed woke up Sunday morning with Jonathan's soft, full lips wrapped around the solid head of his penis. Jonathan was under the covers, on his knees between Ed's legs, squeezing Ed's nuts with his right hand while he sucked the head. Ed spread his legs, shifted his head higher on the pillow, and reached under the covers to force Jonathan's head all the way down.

But he didn't have to press hard. He just rested his palm lightly on Jonathan's crown and in less than a second his erection was hitting the back of Jonathan's throat. Ed closed his eyes and groaned. He had had his fair share of blow jobs, but he'd never met anyone who knew how to suck dick like Jonathan. (Not even Jake. And that was something Ed would never have admitted out loud.) Jonathan had a way of sucking and creating a vacuum of pressure that triggered every nerve ending in Ed's penis. Ed wasn't sure exactly how he did this, but it felt like he used his tongue, his lips and the sides of his face to create what felt more like an articulate hand job than a blow job. The inside of his mouth was warm and wet and mushy. His teeth never grated or irritated the shaft; he never gagged. He maintained a steady rhythm. Jonathan could suck with the same even beat without stopping to rest for air or relief until Ed was ready to explode.

Ed wanted a blow job that morning. He just wanted to lie there without moving. He pulled the covers off and smiled at Jonathan. "Can I come like this?" he asked.

Jonathan stopped sucking. He lifted his eyes and nodded yes, then he closed them again and went back to work.

Ed spread his legs and stretched them out. He pointed his toes, put his hands behind his head, and closed his eyes. Ed knew Jonathan wanted to please him, and Ed was ready to deliver.

A few minutes later, Ed's body tightened and he said, "I'm close."

Jonathan grabbed his own erection without breaking the rhythm. He jerked his own penis and sucked at the same time. Ed's balls tightened and his right leg moved up and down a few times. Then he grunted, leaned forward, and said, "Ah yes, I'm coming. Here it comes."

It was a smooth, powerful climax that left post-orgasmic sensations drifting through his body. His shoulders jerked forward and his feet went up an inch off the bed. Jonathan continued to suck until there was nothing left to drain from his penis. And when he finally stopped sucking and removed Ed from his mouth, he squeezed the shaft hard to see if there was anything he'd missed. A small white drop formed at the tip. Jonathan wrapped his swollen lips around the head and sucked that down, too.

Ed closed his eyes and smiled while Jonathan finished him off. He'd once come across a peculiar Web site by accident called Weeping Cock where nasty prudes laughed at sex scenes in films and books about people who enjoyed good sex. He was smiling because it felt like his cock *was* actually weeping. Ed had a funny feeling that the frigid bitches from *Weeping Cock* had never given a good blow job and probably had no idea what it was like for a man to have a guy like Jonathan drain his weeping, dripping cock dry.

When Jonathan finally let go of Ed's dick, he lifted his head and said, "I'll get you a rag." He'd jerked off all over Ed's leg.

"Don't bother," Ed said. "Let's just take a shower together. We have to get up anyway because Noah and Lisa are coming over for brunch, then we're going to this surprise birthday gift thing with Frank and Greg." Noah and Lisa were also moving back into the house that day, and they were coming with all their things, plus two dogs in tow.

Jonathan smiled. "Can we pee in the shower?"

Ed sat up and laughed. "We can do anything you want." This was one of the little things he liked about being with Jonathan. He had a good sense of humor. Neither one of them was particularly kinky, nor were they into raunchy sex of any kind. But Ed knew how much Jonathan liked to hold his penis while he peed in the shower. He didn't want Ed to pee on him—God forbid—he just wanted to hold it and guide the stream down the drain.

* * * *

When Noah, Lisa, and the dogs arrived, the house came to life again. Jonathan remained in the kitchen preparing brunch and Ed helped them carry their belongings up to their rooms. Noah had decided to name the new puppy *Finder*, because he truly believed that he'd brought them good luck and that he'd helped them *find* Tucker. But Ed thought he should have called him *Biter*, because all he did was nip and bite at poor Tucker's feet to get attention. But Tucker took it in stride. Ed had given him an exam and a clean bill of health, even if he the dog was just a little slower now. He'd let Finder go just so far, then he'd bark once and Finder's tail would go between his legs and he'd back off.

Jonathan prepared eggs Benedict and blueberry waffles. He made them from scratch and he was so neat that the kitchen didn't even look like anyone had been cooking. There were no stains or water marks on the glass cook top and no dirty pots and pans in the sink. Ed just scratched the back of his head and smiled. If he'd been cooking, they would have had to sandblast the glass cook top and empty the sink with plastic gloves.

While they were eating, Jonathan said, "I've been offered a

new job. You all know Greg is a producer at a local TV station, and he wants me to take a job as a co-anchor on the six o'clock news." His voice was quiet. He stared down at his plate as if he was scared to look up and see Ed's reaction.

Lisa dropped her fork. "Are you serious?"

Jonathan nodded and took a bite of a waffle.

"What about your own TV show?" Ed asked. This was all news to him. He didn't know Greg had offered Jonathan a job in San Francisco. He thought Jonathan was going back to New York at the end of the week, and Ed had been avoiding the subject.

Jonathan shrugged his shoulders. "I didn't say anything to anyone because I wanted to think about it," he said, "but I found out *Dream Away* was canceled by the network." He looked at Ed and smiled. "Your house is the last show we'll ever do."

Lisa grabbed his hand and said, "I'm so sorry, Jonathan. You should have said something."

"Ah well," Ed said, "I'm sorry too." But he really wasn't sorry. The thought of Jonathan going back to New York had been making him crazy. But he wasn't sure what to do about it.

He smiled. "I'm fine with it. The show's been on the air for five years and the ratings have been good. It's time to end it, and I'm doing it with a really good show thanks to Ed and Noah. And the network wants to sign me to a three-year contract, at twice the money I'm getting now, for a new show they plan to do this fall."

"Well, that's good news," Lisa said. But when she saw Jonathan wasn't smiling she added, "Isn't it?"

"I'm not sure," Jonathan said. "I know that I'd be a fool to turn down an offer for twice the money and all that national exposure. But the new show sounds really cheesy and sensational. I was considering it but I didn't expect Greg to offer me a job yesterday at the party. I'd have to take a significant cut in pay, and I'd have to relocate to San Francisco."

When Noah heard he might be moving to San Francisco for good, he jumped off his seat and started to clap his hands. "Take the news job," he shouted. "You can be here all the time then. And I can see you on the news every night."

Lisa squeezed Jonathan's hand. "How do you feel about all this?"

Jonathan shrugged. "I was a journalism major in college, and I originally wanted to work in TV news or in print journalism. But I got sidetracked with *Dream Away*. The money was good, and the show was a hit." He looked directly at Ed and said, "I'm just not sure what to do. I have to give Greg an answer this week."

Ed knew Jonathan was looking at him. But Ed didn't know what to say. He wanted Jonathan to stay in San Francisco, but the words were stuck in his throat. Ed had finally started to sleep again, and Noah was smiling and laughing for the first time in over a year. Jonathan had given them life without even trying too hard. But Ed couldn't stop thinking about Jake. He felt guilty, as if he were betraying his memory or cheating on him. Ed knew it wasn't rational, but he couldn't help the way he felt.

So he stood from the table without saying a word and crossed to the back door. He slapped his thigh and grabbed two leashes from a hook next to the door. Then he called the dogs and said, "I'm going to take them both out for a long walk. Frank and Greg will be here soon and these dogs both need to go out and get some exercise. They'll be alone for a while today."

Lisa put her hands on her hips and glared at Ed. "What do *you* think Jonathan should do, *Ed?*" she asked. She was tapping her foot and pointing a butter knife. Ed hadn't seen that expression on her face since Hillary Clinton lost the primary.

Jonathan stood from the table slowly and started to clear the dirty dishes. He turned his back to them and refused to look at Ed.

Ed hooked Finder and Tucker to their leashes and stood up. He knew what Lisa was doing. She was putting him on the spot and he wasn't going to stand for it. This was none of her business. He shrugged his shoulders and said, "I'll be back in a few minutes." Then he opened the back door and went outside as if he hadn't even heard her question.

But when the door was shut and no one could hear him, he looked up at the blue sky and said, "If I could just have a sign, Jake. I'm not asking for much. Just a sign that you're okay with Jonathan and you're okay with me moving on with someone else."

Ed wasn't a religious man and he wasn't into anything paranormal. But he'd always had a feeling Jake was watching over him, and he figured it couldn't hurt to ask.

By the time he came back, the kitchen was clean and Greg and Frank were in the front hall waiting for them. Noah was fidgeting and asking questions about where they were going, but Frank and Greg refused to tell him. Jonathan was quiet and wouldn't look Ed in the eye.

It was like that all the way to Sonoma. They took Ed's Range Rover because Frank's and Greg's car was too small for everyone. Noah sat in the third-row seat. (Range Rovers don't come with a third-row seat, but Ed had found a vendor who knew how to make one that faced backwards, and Noah loved it). Lisa, Frank, and Greg sat in the back seat. Ed and Jonathan sat up front. Frank gave Ed directions to where they were going, and Noah continued to ask Greg questions about the surprise. They made a guessing game of it to pass the time. But Greg refused to tell him. "I'll give you three clues," Greg said. "One, I know you're a huge fan of this because you've told me you are. Two, it's something very colorful and not many people do it. And three, you'll probably want to do it again in the future."

"That's no fair," Noah said. "That could be anything. It could be a cupcake."

Greg laughed. "Sorry, it's not a cupcake, and that's all I can say right now. You'll find out soon enough."

But now Ed was curious about this colossal, childish secret they were keeping. It was pissing him off. Ed hated surprises and he was only going along with this for Noah's sake. If it had been up to him, Frank and Greg would have told him where they were going or they wouldn't have gone at all. So Ed gripped the steering wheel and frowned all the way to Sonoma. Jonathan sat there, without saying a word, staring out the window. Ed knew Jonathan was mad at him for avoiding Lisa's question. He was slumped over in the seat and he was pouting.

At one point during the drive Ed pointed to a vineyard on the right, and said, "That's beautiful."

Jonathan just grunted and whispered, "It's very nice. I'm sure they make nice wine."

"This is the first time I've ever been to wine country," Ed said.

Jonathan grunted again and said, "Isn't that nice. I'm sure you'll like it."

Ed smiled. "Is this the first time you've been here?"

Jonathan turned and faced him. He lowered his eyebrows and gave him a look. He didn't say a word; he just lifted one eyebrow and glared. Then he straightened his shoulders, adjusted his back to the seat, and stared out through the windshield. He pressed his lips together so tightly they pinched and puckered.

Ed sighed and shook his head. All he wanted was one little sign. Was that too much to ask?

When they reached a long gravel road lined with a white horse fence, Frank told Ed to turn left. He drove slowly; the road had to be at least a mile long. It was lined with tall, established trees that had been planted in perfect, identical rows. They weren't surrounded by thick circles of mulch and they could see lumps of imperfect roots bulging to the surface of the grass. Beyond the trees were long stretches of lush, green grass, the kind of grass that grew thick and natural on its own without that dark, chemically treated look Ed had noticed in so many housing developments in the suburbs.

As they rounded a bend and Ed veered to the left, the road opened up to another vast field of green grass. To the left there was a small, beige building that looked like an office. There were a few cars parked out front and there was a small sign over the front door that he couldn't read.

Frank shouted, "We're here. You can park on the side of the building next to the station wagon."

Ed pulled up next to a green station wagon and switched off the motor. Then he got out so he could open the back door for Noah. He'd never seen him so excited. Noah was jumping in his seat and looking back and forth. And when Ed opened the door, Noah bolted from the car and ran up to Jonathan. "What's the surprise? Where are we?"

Jonathan shrugged his shoulders and looked at Frank. Frank and Greg were both smiling.

But before they had a chance to answer him, there was a strange noise. Noah pointed to the sky and shouted, "It's a balloon. Is this our present? Is this the surprise?"

Greg put his hand on Noah's shoulder and said, "We know how much you love balloon rides. We figured it would be the perfect gift for you and Lisa. We're all going up, and you're going to see San Francisco like you've never seen it before."

But Noah stopped smiling. He stepped back and said, "I don't know about this. My Dad doesn't like heights and he might not like this too much."

Everyone turned and faced Ed. But Ed was looking up at the sky and watching the most beautiful hot air balloon he'd ever seen cross over their heads. It was gliding down toward the field, on its way to a graceful landing in the middle of the grass. It was pale blue-green, as close to Waterbury Green as any color could get, and there were thin gold and white stripes on four sides.

Lisa frowned and walked up to Ed's side. "I know how you feel about heights, Ed. Please be nice. Frank and Greg meant well."

Ed looked down at her and shook his head a few times. Then he smiled and lifted her off the ground. He held her and turned around and around, shouting, "I love it. It's the best present ever. It's a balloon, of all things. It's a freaking balloon."

Lisa's eyes widened and she held his shoulders for support. "Have you lost your mind, Ed?" she asked.

The rest of them watched Ed going around in circles with Lisa. Their mouths were open and they looked like they were afraid to move.

Then he put her down and jogged to where Noah was standing. He squatted down and grabbed Noah's shoulders. "I'm going up this time, buddy," he said. "We're all going up. I'm not afraid anymore." He lifted his arms and shook his fists to the sky. "I'm not afraid."

Noah smiled and ran to hug him. "Thanks, Dad," he said. Then he turned back to the others and shouted, "Let's go."

Noah ran to the other side of the field where the balloon was landing. The others followed, but Ed reached for Jonathan's arm and said, "Wait. I want to say something."

Jonathan was giving him the silent treatment and he was still pouting. He pulled his arm back fast, but he stopped walking to listen to what Ed had to say. He put his hands in his pockets and stared down at his shoes.

"Don't leave," Ed said. "I love you and I want you to stay here with us. The thought of you going back to New York makes me crazy."

Jonathan lifted his head and blinked a few times. "Are you serious? Because I don't want to leave. I want to stay here with you and Noah and Tucker and Finder. I don't care about my new contract or the money. I don't want to host a sleazeball show called *Robbing the Cradle*. I want to take the job at the TV station. It's what I've always wanted to do. But most of all, I want to stay because I've never loved anyone like I love you, Ed. You're the dream and the fantasy I never thought would come true."

Ed smiled and spread his arms apart. "I'm just an ordinary vet and a big slob," he said. "I hope you know what you're getting into."

Jonathan went to him and put his arms around his shoulders. "But you're my big slob," he said, "And for the first time in my life I know what I'm doing. Then he kissed him on the lips and said, "I love you so much. I still can't believe I had to come all the way to San Francisco to find you."

Ed closed his eyes and held him so hard he lifted him up off the grass. When he opened his eyes a minute later and raised his head, he looked over Jonathan's shoulder and saw everyone was standing in front of the balloon, watching them. They were all smiling, including Noah, and they were clapping their hands.

He put Jonathan down and said, "Let's go. This is the first time I've ever been up in one of these things and I'm glad it's with you."

Then he put his arm around Jonathan's shoulders and they crossed to where the others were standing. On the way there, Ed looked up at the sky and whispered, "Thank you, Jake."

THE END